TRAIL OF DANGER

Suddenly the woods were filled with the booming sound of cracking ice and melting clumps of snow, but there was something else, too. There was the sound of wood breaking, and rocks skittering and crashing against one another. Stevie's mind raced even faster than her horse galloped. There was only one thing it could be. There were rocks rolling down the hill! It had to be the rock formation Dinah had been talking about. It was like an avalanche, and Dinah was riding right into the most dangerous part of it!

Then, thirty yards in front of her, Dinah's horse reared. It was a sight that Stevie would never forget. . . .

THE SADDLE CLUB

SNOW
RIDE

BONNIE BRYANT

A BANTAM SKYLARK BOOK®
NEW YORK · TORONTO · LONDON · SYDNEY · AUCKLAND

I would like to give special thanks to Lou Willett Stanek for her help on this book.
—B.B.

RL 5, 009–012

SNOW RIDE
A Bantam Skylark Book / February 1992

Skylark Books is a registered trademark of Bantam Books,
a division of Bantam Doubleday Dell Publishing Group, Inc.
Registered in U.S. Patent and Trademark Office and elsewhere.

"The Saddle Club" is a trademark of Bonnie Bryant Hiller.
The Saddle Club design/logo, which consists of an inverted
U-shaped design, a riding crop, and a riding hat is a
trademark of Bantam Books.

ISBN 0-553-15907-0

Published simultaneously in the United States and Canada

Bantam Books are published by Bantam Books, a division of Bantam Doubleday Dell Publishing Group, Inc. Its trademark,
consisting of the words "Bantam Books" and the portrayal of a
rooster, is Registered in U.S. Patent and Trademark Office and in
other countries. Marca Registrada. Bantam Books, 666 Fifth Ave-
nue, New York, New York 10103.

PRINTED IN THE UNITED STATES OF AMERICA

OPM   0 9 8 7 6 5 4 3 2 1

STEVIE LAKE TOOK a deep breath. It was spring in Virginia. The air was fresh and warm. Wisps of clouds stretched across the bright blue sky. Early wildflowers peeked up through the rich earth. These things made her very happy. Warm weather meant more outdoor horseback riding. More horseback riding also meant more time to spend with her two best friends, Carole Hanson and Lisa Atwood. The three girls were walking together to Stevie's house from Pine Hollow Stable, where they had just been riding.

"I think when I finish training Starlight, he's going to be the best jumper in the county," Carole said, interrupting Stevie's thoughts of horseback riding with thoughts of her own. Starlight was Carole's horse. Carole thought he had championship potential. Her friends agreed. After their riding class, Stevie and Lisa had watched and encouraged Starlight while Carole worked with him on jumps.

Stevie recalled the way Starlight soared over jumps. "It's like he's learning to fly," she observed. "Only he doesn't just want to fly. He wants to make it into orbit!"

As the three girls walked along, they continued chatting happily about their favorite subject: horses. They loved horses so much that they had formed The Saddle Club. It was a club with only two rules. The first one was that all members had to be horse crazy. The second one was that all members had to be willing to help one another out no matter what the problem was: horseback riding, school, boys, or anything.

The three of them could hardly have been more different from one another. Carole was black-haired, with deep brown eyes and a light brown complexion. Of the three of them, she'd been riding the longest. She'd been brought up on Marine Corps bases where her father was a colonel, and she'd learned to ride in the military stables. She planned a career with horses, but she couldn't decide what it would be. She couldn't choose among owner, breeder, rider, and veterinarian. Most of the time she was convinced she wanted to do all of those. Her friends thought she'd probably manage it. Carole could be flaky and indecisive about a lot of things, but never about horses. If horses were involved, Carole was all business.

Lisa was a year older than Carole and Stevie but didn't look it. She had long brown hair and a young face. Her creamy complexion gave her a look of total innocence. Lisa was superorganized and was good at just about everything she did. She always got A's in school, and she was always the president of something there. Her mother sometimes wished that Lisa had put her mind to a more ladylike activity than horseback riding, something like ballet or playing the violin. Lisa was pretty good at those, too, but her heart was in horseback riding.

Stevie was the most mischievous of the threesome. She had long light brown hair and hazel eyes. There was a random collection of freckles scattered across the bridge of her nose and her cheeks seemed to reflect the mischief that sparkled in her eyes. If there was trouble around, Stevie found a way to get into it. And, usually, if Stevie was in trouble, her friends were right in there with her. More than once Stevie had been awfully glad for The Saddle Club rule about having to help your friends. She'd really needed it! One of her strongest areas as a rider was dressage—the most disciplined kind of riding there was for a horse. Most of the time, however, "undisciplined" was a word Stevie heard a lot of, from Max Regnery, her riding instructor, from the headmistress of her school, from her teachers, from her parents—even from her three brothers. Yet Stevie always seemed to manage to come out on top. It was one of the things her friends loved most about her.

"I used to think you had to be almost lying along the horse's neck, instead of just parallel to it, before he'd jump correctly," Stevie remarked, returning to the subject of Starlight's jumping ability.

"You can do that," Carole joked. "Especially if you want to fly out of the saddle."

"Ah yes. That was the lesson I learned in my first jump!" Stevie said, recalling how she'd ended up in the dirt. "I can remember how that horse stopped to look at me. I thought he was laughing."

"He probably was," Carole agreed. "But the thing about training—either a horse or a rider—is that you have to keep on teaching the lessons until they become automatic. There are no shortcuts. Those are always mistakes. If you don't do something right, then the only thing you and the horse learn is how to make a mistake."

"Uh-oh, here she goes," Lisa said. Stevie smiled. So did Carole. Carole was famous for giving long-winded answers about horses to questions nobody had asked. Her friends teased her about it, but the fact was, they were usually glad when she shared her considerable knowledge.

"Okay, okay, so enough about horses," Carole replied.

"I'll change the subject. Let's talk about riding. Spring vacation starts next week. How much riding are we going to do?"

"A lot," Lisa said. "My parents have said I could ride every day. And you know what I was thinking? Why don't we plan a trail ride before class on the Saturday at the end of vacation?"

"Great!" Stevie said enthusiastically. "We can—uh-oh . . ."

"What's the matter?" Carole asked.

"Saturday, Saturday . . . ," Stevie said thoughtfully. "That's the nineteenth, right?"

"Yup," Lisa confirmed.

"That's the day of Phil's pony club meeting. They're having an unmounted meeting, and he asked me to come to it."

Phil Marston was Stevie's boyfriend. He was also an out-of-town member of The Saddle Club. He and Stevie had met at riding camp and formed a close friendship because of the love they shared for riding. They were both naturally competitive as well. When the girls' pony club, Horse Wise, played games against Phil's pony club, Cross County, sparks flew.

"I can't imagine why he wants me to come to the meeting," Stevie continued. "He usually wants to keep all the things they do secret from me. Something's up."

"Maybe he just wants to spend some time with you," Lisa suggested.

Stevie smiled. "Maybe," she agreed. "Then again, maybe not. Anyway, I have to wait until the nineteenth to find out. I can't even call him and try to squeeze the information out of him. He's on a class trip until Monday. I hate secrets, you know—unless of course I'm in on them!"

"How can you stand the suspense?" Lisa asked a little sarcastically.

"You know the old poem?" Stevie asked. Her friends waited. "'Patience is a virtue; Have it if you can. Seldom in a woman—*Never* in a man.' That's me, Miss Patience."

Both Carole and Lisa burst into laughter. If there was one thing Stevie *didn't* have, it was patience.

The girls were still laughing when they arrived at Stevie's house and took the kitchen by storm. Within minutes they'd located everything they needed for snacks, piled the goodies onto several plates, tucked soda cans into their pockets for carrying ease, and retreated toward Stevie's room, ducking brothers as they went.

They only paused momentarily so Stevie could fetch a letter taped to the door of her room. She didn't have any free hands, so she tugged it loose from the tape with her teeth and dropped it on her bed.

"Oh, wow!" she said. "It's from Dinah Slattery in Vermont! Remember her?"

Lisa shook her head. "Never heard of her."

"She was at Pine Hollow before you started riding," Carole said. "She used to ride Barq, and Max always had to remind her to keep her heels down. . . ."

"Right," Stevie said, putting the snack foods and the sodas on her bedside table. She picked up Dinah's letter. "She was in our riding class, but she also went to my school, and we used to sit next to one another in art class and draw horses."

"Oh, cool," Lisa said. She loved to draw horses.

"I thought so, too, but the teacher, Miss Eberley, didn't agree. See, we were supposed to be drawing grapes, so when she complained, we just explained that we were drawing an exotic and rare fruit—the equine grape."

"I bet that got her mad," Lisa said.

"It sure did. And it got us a free pass to the principal's office. I think that was the time. Or maybe we got sent to the principal's office the time we got into a meatball fight in the lunchroom. No, it wasn't then, it was . . ."

While Stevie continued to muse out loud, she slit the envelope open and began reading to herself. She considered it a real skill that she could read and talk about different things at the same time.

". . . when John Richman told the teacher we'd fed

the hamster some tuna salad from the lunchroom to see if it caused cancer, and the teacher *believed* him . . . Wow! Guess what?" Stevie said. Suddenly all her attention was riveted on Dinah's letter.

"What?" Lisa and Carole asked in a single voice.

"She's invited me to Vermont! Get this"—then she read out loud—"'Every year, at the time of spring break, we have sugaring off. That's when we collect the sap from the maple trees and make syrup and sugar. We make up teams of three and I just learned that my team is one person short. Naturally, I thought of you. It's a whole week full of fun. We do it the old-fashioned way, using horse-drawn sleds and everything. You're going to love it, Stevie. It's a great time of year here, and I promise we won't spend a minute of it in the principal's office!'"

"Fabulous!" Lisa said. The idea of riding in snowy woods in Vermont was so overwhelming that she couldn't think of anything more to say about it.

Carole could. She jumped up off Stevie's bed and bounded over to where Stevie was still standing and began clapping her on the back. "Oh, it's great! You'll have a wonderful time!"

"Sure," Stevie said. "Except for one thing. Who says I'm going to get to go? After all, my parents are going to insist on having something to say about this—including how much it's going to cost. I can hear them now. In one word. And that word is *no*."

As if on cue, Stevie's mother knocked on the door and stuck her head into Stevie's room. "Can I come in?" she asked.

"Sure," Stevie said. "We'd love to have you join us." She didn't want to be accused of rudeness when she was about to ask her mother a gigantic favor. "Besides, there's something I need to ask you about. Would you like a cookie? Some soda?"

"This is going to be good, isn't it?" Mrs. Lake said brightly, accepting the snack and sitting comfortably in the chair Stevie offered her. Stevie even shooed her cat, Madonna, out of the chair. Stevie's parents had come to enjoy those times when Stevie wanted something. Stevie was a very creative convincer and not above bribery.

"I had a letter from Dinah Slattery," Stevie began.

"I know," her mother said. "And it would be a pleasure to sit here and let you try to convince me you should go to Vermont for the sugaring off. But I don't really have time. I have a brief I have to work on." Stevie's mother was a busy and successful attorney and she often brought work home. "So before you describe all the garden chores you'll do this spring, or how you'll paint the ceiling of the den all by yourself, or how you promise to do extra-credit work in Spanish, *and* change the cat's litter box, I might as well tell you that Mrs. Slattery called me at the office today. Your father and I have already discussed this, and the answer is yes."

"Yes?" Stevie echoed.

"Yes."

Stevie was so astonished that she actually asked, "Why?"

Her mother smiled. "I'm not surprised that you wonder, but it's really very simple. You and your brothers are all out of school next week and your father's been talking about taking you fly-fishing—"

"Uch!" Stevie said.

"My sentiments exactly," Mrs. Lake said. "The problem is that I have this big case coming up, and I can't take time off. Since the boys are getting a trip with your father, it seems only fair that you get a trip, too. So you're going to Vermont." Mrs. Lake stood up and looked at the unopened soda can and the cookies that she still held. "Here," she said. "I can't really accept these. It amounts to bribery after the fact, and that begins to look like extortion. Whoops, I'm sounding like a lawyer instead of a mother. Anyway, you'll leave this Saturday and come back on Sunday a week later. I know you'll have a wonderful time. We'll talk about this some more at dinner, okay? Good-bye, girls," Mrs. Lake said, and then she slipped out the door.

There was a stunned silence in the room.

"Pinch me," Stevie said. Her friends obliged willingly. Then Lisa gave Stevie a big excited hug, and Carole jumped on the bed.

"It's going to be great!" Carole said. "Imagine—a whole week in Vermont!"

"Yeah, the entire vaca—I can't go," Stevie said, a sudden realization coming to her. She sat down on her bed.

"Why not?" Lisa asked, dropping down next to her.

Carole sat on Stevie's other side. "Yeah, why not?" she asked.

"I promised Phil I'd go to the pony club meeting on Saturday. He made me promise, you know. Like it was really important. He's my boyfriend, and a promise is a promise."

Lisa and Carole looked at one another.

Lisa wrinkled her brows. "Sure," she agreed, "but a trip to Vermont is a whole trip to Vermont, and a pony club meeting is just a meeting. Phil will understand. Call him." Lisa pointed to the phone on Stevie's bedside table.

"That's just it," Stevie said. "I can't. Remember the class trip? I can't reach him until Monday, and by then I'll already be in Vermont. I couldn't call him from there. The whole situation is impossible. I'll just have to let Dinah know I can't come." Stevie was only half joking, and her friends knew it.

"Um, Stevie," Carole said. "I think you ought to go to Vermont. I got the distinct impression from what your mother said that if you don't go to Vermont, you'll end up fly-fishing with your brothers and your father, and you'll miss Phil's pony club meeting anyway."

Stevie's face brightened. "Then I'll just have to go to Vermont," she said. "But what about Phil?"

"I'll call him for you on Monday," Lisa offered. "I'm sure if I explain, he'll understand." That was all the convincing Stevie needed, so for the next two hours the girls had a wonderful time discussing the clothes Stevie should take and everything she would need to know about driving a sled pulled by a horse.

2

". . . SO, THE MOST important part seems to be keeping an even tension on the long reins," Stevie told the man in the seat next to her on the plane. Before they had left Washington, he'd expressed some interest in the fact that Stevie was going to be involved in sugaring off, so Stevie had been talking about it ever since the plane had taxied down the runway. Stevie looked out the window as she spoke. They were about to land.

"Oh, my goodness, we're almost here!" she said.

The man sat upright. "In Vermont already?" he asked, looking across Stevie and through the window. He rubbed his eyes. "I had a great nap. I always sleep well on planes. Now, what was it you said you were coming up here to do?"

Stevie felt her mouth drop open. The man had slept through every word she'd said! This called for an appropriate response.

"I said I'm going to be deep-sea diving as part of an archaeological exploration of the underwater caves that housed the early Viking settlers who actually turned out to be the first cousins of Kublai Khan's publicity men who gave the recipe for spaghetti to Marco Polo. We want to see if we can find the part of the recipe that includes sauce. You probably think I'm too young to be involved in something like that, but I'm actually forty-three years old. I just look young."

The man didn't say another word to Stevie. That was all right with her. As the plane descended, she enjoyed looking out the window at the hilly white world below dotted with dark spots that she recognized as evergreens.

Dinah and her father were waiting for Stevie at the gate. It was great to see her after such a long time. Dinah had moved away almost two years before. It wasn't hard to recognize her, though. She was the girl who was leaping up and down excitedly and pointing and waving all at the same time. Stevie hurried through the gate and ran over to Dinah so she could give her a hug.

"You're finally here!" Dinah said.

"I sure am, now where's this maple stuff you've been talking about?"

"Right this way," Dinah said. She took Stevie's carryall

and handed it to her father. He grinned good-naturedly and followed the girls to the luggage claim area. Within a few minutes the three of them were in the Slatterys' car. Mr. Slattery drove while Dinah talked a mile a minute, telling Stevie everything there was to know about sugaring off.

"We can only do it at this time of year," she explained. "See, it has to be when the days are warm enough for the sap to flow and the nights are cold enough to freeze it. So our job is to go get as much as we can in the daytime."

"Sounds perfectly logical to me," Stevie said, "only I can't figure out where the spigot is. What do we do? Twist off a branch?"

"Ha ha, very funny," Dinah said. "No, what we do is we make a hole. We drill it. Then we put a spigot—only it's called a spile—into the hole. It's a tube that fits into the hole and redirects the sap out of the tree into the bucket we hang on the spile. It's all very clever and works very well."

"That's all there is to maple syrup?" Stevie asked. "We just go get it from the tree?"

"No way!" answered Dinah. "What we get from the tree is sap. That's like very watery syrup. In fact, you can taste it and you'll hardly be able to figure out what it is. No, what we do then is boil it. And boil it. And boil it. Depending on how you like it, it takes about fifty gallons of sap to make one gallon of syrup. Then, if you want maple sugar, you just keep on boiling. It's a lot of work, but it's worth it, believe me. As far as I'm concerned, there's nothing sweeter and more wonderful than maple syrup and sugar."

"This is all fine and good," Stevie said. "But what does it have to do with horses? I distinctly remember your saying that your riding class was doing this."

"Oh, that's the best part of all," Dinah told her. "And it's where you really come into the picture. See, our stable owns the Sugar Hut. The owner, Mr. Daviet, bought all the land at once for his stable and only discovered later that it was covered with sugar maples. So he named the place Sugarbush, built the Sugar Hut as well as the stable, and started this sort of off-shoot business. It's mostly for fun, and the best part is what our riding class is doing. See, we've divided up into teams of three for a competition. The team that collects the most sap—and then makes the most syrup—wins the grand prize. When Mr. Daviet announced our teams and told us the rules, he didn't say a thing about not having other friends help. So when my team was only two because of odd numbers, I figured we deserved a little bit of assistance from you. We're sure to cop the grand prize!"

Images of trips to Hawaii, million-dollar checks, and dream vacation houses popped into Stevie's head. Somehow she didn't think that's what this was about. "What's the grand prize?"

"The winning team will always have first pick of riding horses at classes all next summer!"

"Outstanding!" Stevie said, and she meant it. Being able to ride your favorite horse for every class was a real prize. "Let's get started right away—don't want to waste a minute."

"I was hoping you'd feel that way," Dinah said. "See, it's perfect weather for setting out the buckets because it's still pretty cold. Later in the week, the weather is supposed to warm up and the sap will be flowing like crazy. So all we have to do is drop your suitcase off at my house and we'll walk over to the Sugar Hut. You can meet Betsy Hale, who is my teammate for the competition, and we can get started."

"Today?"

"No time like the present!"

It had been a long time since Stevie had seen Dinah, and now she remembered why it was that she'd liked her so much in the first place. They both thought the same way. They were both clever and mischievous and eager to get going on anything that was going to be fun, no matter how much hard work it might be, and no matter how devious they were going to have to be to accomplish it.

Stevie and Dinah stayed at the Slattery house only long enough for Stevie to take her suitcase upstairs and change into jeans and boots. The girls both donned warm winter jackets, hats, scarves, and mittens. Then they were ready to go.

The Sugar Hut turned out to be almost exactly that. It was little more than a hut, but immediately Stevie decided that she loved it. It was a log cabin with a large central chimney. Sweet-smelling smoke curled out of the chimney. Stevie stopped and took a deep breath. "I think I'm going to love this."

"I know you are," Dinah assured her.

There was a girl their age standing by the door of the Sugar Hut. As soon as she spotted Stevie and Dinah, she waved cheerfully. "There you are!" she greeted them. "You must be Stevie, right?"

"Right," Stevie confirmed.

"This is Betsy," Dinah introduced her.

"Ah, our partner in crime," Stevie said, looking at the girl. She had dark brown hair that curled up around her cap. Her face was round. She had deep brown eyes and a quirky smile that made dimples on her cheeks. Stevie liked her immediately.

"So what's going on now?" Dinah asked. "Are we ready to start?"

"Mr. Daviet has been sending out teams on snow-shoes," Betsy said.

"That's how we go out when we first put in the spiles," Dinah explained. "Snowshoes are hard to walk in and slow, but that's the way the competition works."

"Yeah, well, everybody but us has to go out on snowshoes," Betsy said.

"Yes?" Dinah asked.

Betsy's eyes were sparkling mischievously. Stevie knew the look. She'd worn it often enough herself.

"Well, see, I explained to Mr. Daviet about this friend you had visiting, and I told him all about the fact that she was somewhat lame. . . ."

Betsy and Dinah looked at Stevie. She obligingly slung an arm across Dinah's shoulder and started limping.

"What's the matter with me?" Stevie asked. She was doing a fairly good imitation of the Hunchback of Notre Dame, favoring her right leg.

Betsy giggled. "That's what Mr. Daviet asked," she said. "I had to think fast, too. The first thing that came into my head was that you'd thrown a shoe, but I knew he wouldn't fall for that. I just told him you were recovering from surgery. It seemed to sort of cover everything. At first, he said that if you were so sick, you shouldn't be in the woods, so I told him you were nearly all recovered."

Stevie took her arm off Dinah's shoulder and modified her limp. Now she looked more like Tiny Tim, favoring her left leg.

"Perfect," Betsy declared.

"Okay, now that my injury's settled, what's it going to do for us?" Stevie asked.

"It's getting us a horse-drawn sled," Betsy said. "Now we don't have to use the snowshoes. We'll get a big head start on all the other riders because they have to walk, and we can ride. My sister's going to be here in just a few minutes with the sled."

"Your sister? What's she got to do with it?" Stevie asked.

"Her sister is Jodi," Dinah explained. "Jodi is the stable hand who works for Mr. Daviet. She's a great rider—"

"She's not all that great," Betsy interrupted.

"Well, she's better than we are, and she gets to spend all of her time at the stable—"

"—except for the time she *says* she's at the stable, when she's really with a boyfriend," Betsy added.

"And she helps in class and she can ride whenever she wants to and she told me that she'd take me on the Rocky Road Trail one of these days," Dinah said.

It was clear that Dinah and Betsy were very similar in many ways and agreed about almost everything except about Betsy's sister Jodi. Stevie didn't have any sisters. She had only brothers. She had the feeling, though, that Betsy felt the same way about her sister that Stevie did about her brothers (i.e., that they were quite unnecessary to a satisfactory life). Stevie decided she'd make up her own mind about Jodi when the time came.

Her thoughts were interrupted by a strangely familiar sound. It was a sound Stevie had heard only once before in her life—on the Starlight Ride at Pine Hollow on Christmas Eve when Max and his mother had ridden through the field on a horse-drawn sleigh. It was the sound of sleigh bells!

Stevie stopped and turned around. There, coming along the wooded road, was a flatbed sleigh, drawn by a large workhorse. An older girl held the reins, and every time she flicked them, the bells on the leather rang out their song.

Stevie had the wonderful feeling that she'd just traveled backward in time a century or two and was in colonial Vermont and she liked it very much. She just wished Carole and Lisa were there to share it.

3

THE SLEIGH DREW to a stop in front of the Sugar Hut, and the older girl got off.

"Here, you take the reins," she said, handing the long leathers to Dinah.

"Me?" Dinah said.

"Yeah," the girl returned. Then, without further ado, she walked back along the snowy path where she'd come from.

"That was Jodi," Betsy explained to Stevie. "My older sister."

"She's usually friendlier," Dinah hastened to add. "I guess she wasn't crazy about the idea of having to hitch up the sleigh for somebody else. That must be why she hurried off. Anyway, you'll meet her again while you're here. I'm sure you'll like her."

"I'm sure," Stevie said, though she felt she would be surer if Jodi had been nicer.

"So much for my sister," Betsy said. "Let's get going now. I want to take advantage of every bit of time we have. After all, a lot's at stake."

"And his name is Goldie," Dinah said. "That's the horse I'm going to use this summer—*if* we win."

"My favorite horse is named Mister, and I *will* ride him. We've just got to win," Betsy said. "So let's get going!"

As far as Stevie was concerned, it was as if a gunshot had started the race. She was raring to go. But they weren't quite ready to leave yet.

First the girls had to collect the gear they would need. They look two large hand drills with big long bits in them. They also took an ample supply of spiles and buckets.

"The more trees we tap, the more syrup we collect," Betsy explained, putting another stack of buckets on the sleigh. "Some of the big old trees we'll tap in two places. That's why we need so many buckets. And the real advantage of not having to use snowshoes is that we can take a zillion buckets on the sleigh at once, and the others can take only what they can load onto a hand-pulled sled."

"But the disadvantage is that, according to the rules, every single bucket we take out we have to set to tap. For each bucket we bring back empty, we have to forfeit one bucket of sap to the other teams," Dinah explained.

"Oh, yeah, right," Betsy said. She regarded the stacks of buckets thoughtfully, estimating their ability to tap the trees. Eventually she decided to remove exactly six buckets from the sleigh.

"How did you figure that out?" Stevie asked.

"Beats me," Betsy confessed. "It just looked like six too many!"

Stevie laughed.

With that, Betsy climbed up in the front of the sleigh and took the reins from Dinah. They were on their way.

The three girls sat together on a wooden bench near the front of the sleigh. Betsy, in the middle, held the reins. She wasn't sitting so much as standing, and she had her feet braced against a board at the front edge of the sleigh. She held one rein in each hand. When they were ready to start, she flicked the reins so they slapped the horse's rump lightly, and she made a clicking sound with the back of her tongue. The horse began walking obediently, pulling the sleigh through the thick spring snow.

At first Stevie was aware of the lumbering motion of the large horse, feeling the separate tugs of each step he took. Then, as the horse began moving more steadily, all she felt was the easy glide of the smooth runners of the sleigh.

It really just confirmed her feeling that she'd traveled backward in time a few hundred years. She shared the thought with Dinah and Betsy.

"Wait until we get to work," Betsy said. "You're going to wish for the twentieth century again!"

Stevie wasn't sure what Betsy meant, but the fact that both Betsy and Dinah seemed to find it funny made her slightly uneasy.

Their first turn was a sharp right off a narrow section of path. Stevie watched with interest as Betsy approached the turn. First she flicked the reins gently to get the horse's attention and then tugged a little on the left rein. The horse swished his tail amiably and moved to the left. The sleigh moved way to the left side of the path as well. Then Betsy tugged on the right rein gently and held it firmly. Slowly the horse turned to the right. The sleigh followed. Soon Betsy released the pressure on the rein, the horse stopped turning, and the sleigh straightened out, heading right along the path they'd wanted.

"That's complicated," Stevie said. "Do you always have to go the opposite way before you turn?"

"Only when it's tight," Betsy explained. "If I try to turn too sharply, I run the risk of having the horse break the shafts on the sleigh or having the shafts hurt the horse." Stevie looked to see what she meant. The shafts were two long pieces of wood, one on either side of the horse, that attached to the sleigh. A sharp turn could be real trouble. It was clear, though, that Betsy knew what she was doing. It made Stevie feel confident.

The woods were crisscrossed with trails, all totally mystifying to Stevie, but Betsy seemed to know where she was going, and when Betsy was in doubt, Dinah came to her rescue. Betsy drove the sleigh surely, directing the horse at each turn and urging him gently when he decided to slow down and examine something interesting.

"Off to the right now," Dinah said. Stevie didn't know how Dinah could remember where to turn or how they'd even gotten where they were.

"That's right," Betsy agreed. She tugged gently on the right rein at a fork in the path. The path rose to the right. The horse followed willingly.

Suddenly they left the woods and came out into an open area that Stevie thought was probably a field in the summer. For the first time since they'd left the Sugar Hut, Stevie could see where they were. They were completely surrounded by forest-covered hills and mountains. Many of the trees, especially on the higher parts of the hills, were evergreens whose bushy branches weighed heavily under blankets of snow. Other trees, now bare of their leaves, stood in stark contrast, with snow on top of their branches, exposed bark below.

"Oh," Stevie said, surprised, and delighted at the wonderful sight that looked as if it had been painted for the occasion by a greeting card company.

Dinah laughed, pleased by Stevie's reaction. "They don't call this place Ver-mont for nothing," she said. "It's from French, you know. The *Ver* means green and the *mont*—"

"Don't tell me. It means mountain," Stevie finished for her.

"Go to the head of the class," Dinah said.

"Nope, go to the back of the sleigh instead," Betsy corrected her. "Because we're almost here, and it's time to get to work."

Betsy gave the reins a final snick to urge the horse across the field. When they reached the edge of the forest, she pulled gently but firmly and brought the horse and the sleigh to a halt.

"Everybody out," she said. She secured the reins to keep the sleigh stopped, and the three girls piled out, ready to start their work. "Come on, now, I'll show you what we do."

Stevie helped unload some of the equipment they'd so recently loaded onto the sleigh. She took a few buckets and some spiles and carried one of the large drills.

Betsy began by examining some of the trees. "I'm looking for the sugar maples," she explained.

Stevie looked at the trees that surrounded them. They

were all tall, they were all bare. They all looked alike. There seemed to be no way to tell any of them apart. Stevie had a sudden image of them going to a lot of work to collect sap from oaks or ashes.

"How can you tell which are the sugar maples?" she asked.

"They're the ones with the sugar maple leaf painted on the bark at eye level," Betsy explained, pointing to the nearest tree.

Stevie blinked, looked again, and then laughed.

"A real naturalist can tell the trees apart when they don't have leaves," Dinah explained, "but it can be kind of risky, so a long time ago they came up with this bright idea of marking the trees in the summer when it's not hard to tell. It saves us a lot of trouble. It also keeps us from ruining a batch of syrup by adding the wrong sap."

"Bingo!" Dinah announced. "Here are three together."

The girls trod over to the trees Dinah had spotted. Betsy took her drill, checked to see that the bit was in tightly, and began the job. She drilled a hole into the trunk of the tree, about three feet above the ground. Stevie watched the wood shavings emerge from the hole, and then when the bit had gone in about an inch and a half, Betsy pulled the drill back out.

"That's it," Betsy said. "That's as far as I need to go." Noticing Stevie's surprise at the shallowness of the hole, she explained that the sap ran right beneath the bark of the tree. Then she poked one of the spiles into the hole she'd drilled, tapped it gently with a hammer, hung a bucket from the spile, put a simple cover over the top of the bucket, and declared the job done—until the next tree.

"That's all there is to it?" Stevie asked.

"That's all until the next tree," Dinah said. "And here's the next tree."

Dinah took her own drill and checked the bit. Then she began drilling. She repeated the procedure exactly as far as Stevie could tell, but she wasn't satisfied.

"I put it in at the wrong angle," she explained, pulling the drill back out. "You've got to angle the drill upward so the sap can flow downward through the spile. Also, it's a good idea to tap right under a big branch. See, a big branch is doing a lot of growing, so the tree will be sending the most sap in that direction." She studied the shape of the tree a little more, judged where the biggest branch was, placed the drill bit on the trunk, and began again. "I don't mind, and it only takes a few minutes, but too many holes punched in the tree can't be good for it," Dinah said. "It also takes valuable time from our tapping."

"Well, just how good can it be for the tree to have us take its sap out anyway?" Stevie asked. She was beginning to feel just a little bit sorry for the trees.

Betsy laughed. "I wondered the same thing the first

time I did this," she said. "I was out here with Mr. Daviet, who has been doing this for practically centuries. Know what he said?"

"What?" Stevie asked.

"'By the size of the trunk on this tree, I'd judge it to be nearly two hundred years old. It's probably been tapped for sap every year of the last hundred and fifty. Doesn't seem to have hurt it much, does it?'"

Stevie looked around her and saw that the maples in the woods were all big old trees, surely veterans of many years of tapping. None of them seemed the worse for being tapped every year. And besides, if nobody tapped the maple trees, how would she ever have the wonderful syrup on her pancakes?

"My turn to try," Stevie said, now more eager than ever to pitch in.

Betsy handed her the drill. It was the big, jointed kind. She put the pointed end against the trunk as her friends had done and braced her body against the round end. She leaned forward toward the tree trunk and began cranking the drill. The blade bit into the trunk.

"It's working!" Stevie declared proudly. The next thing that happened was that the bark of the tree cracked and the bit slid aside. Stevie completely lost her balance and ended up sitting in the snow, the drill hanging limply from where it had caught in the bark on the side of the tree.

"Ah, that's what we call 'getting the hang of it,'" Betsy said, laughing and offering Stevie a hand to help her get up. "The trick is not to push too hard on the drill. It'll slip out every time when you push like that. Now try again."

Stevie didn't like falling down. Looking ridiculous wasn't her favorite activity. She was tempted to hold off trying again because she didn't want to make a fool of herself a second time. But even more, she didn't like the idea that there was something she couldn't do. She took the drill in her hand and began again, a little more cautiously this time.

Betsy stood next to her and coached. "That's right, now begin it gently and slowly. Easy pressure."

Stevie listened and she followed the instructions. They worked. Before too long the drill was cutting straight into the trunk of the tree. A small collection of shavings curled out of the hole in the trunk, drifting down into the snow beneath the drill.

"Now you can put a little more pressure on, but not too much. Let the tool do the work."

That was a familiar idea to Stevie. One of the secrets of riding that she'd learned the hard way was to let the horse do the work. As a rider, what she had to do was tell the horse what she wanted, make sure he understood, and then let him do it. Beginning riders often had the mistaken notion that they had to keep telling the horse everything, all the time. It usually resulted in a kind of "kick and yank" riding that was bad for the horse *and* the rider. Now all she had to do was let the drill do the work—except, of course, she had to keep on cranking it.

"That's deep enough!" Dinah declared, studying the amount of the drill bit that had disappeared into the tree trunk. "You've gotten beneath the bark and into the tree. That's all you need!"

Stevie dropped down to her knees to look for herself. It was unmistakable. She'd done it. She pulled the drill back out of the tree trunk. Proudly she took the spile that Dinah handed her and tapped it into the tree with the hammer Betsy gave her. Then, with some ceremony, she hung a bucket on the spile and placed a cover on the bucket.

"Ta-*dah*!" she cried.

Dinah and Betsy clapped.

"Now let's get back to work," Dinah said.

They found many more trees in the grove by the edge of the field and tapped them all. Then they moved on to another maple grove, and a third. After a while it seemed to Stevie that there was a nearly endless supply of maple trees and perhaps they'd never be done, never use all the buckets they'd brought. That was when she understood what Betsy and Dinah had meant about wishing she was back in the twentieth century. Modern tapping used electric drills and, instead of collecting the sap in buckets, collected it in tubes that went to a central collection point. It was faster and more efficient. However, Stevie thought, it probably wasn't as much fun.

By the time the girls finished tapping every sugar maple they could find in the third grove, they'd used up all but two of their buckets, and it was time to go back in because it was beginning to be dark.

"I can't stand the idea of returning an empty bucket, much less two," Dinah said. "I'm sure we'll find more trees to tap before we get back to the Sugar Hut."

"We may find a couple of trees, but they've got to be convenient," Betsy said sensibly. "After all, we don't want to have to go traipsing all over the place just to empty one or two buckets. Besides, we might forget where they are. That's as bad as forfeiting. So, anyway, let's go."

"I think it's my turn to drive," Dinah said. "I know you love it, *but . . .*"

Betsy smiled. "I do love it," she said, handing the reins to Dinah. "Sometimes I love it so much that I forget that other people like to have a chance. Sorry about that."

Dinah slid into the center spot on the sleigh and took over driving. "Mr. Daviet thinks it's important for all of us to learn to drive a horse on a wagon or sleigh," she told Stevie. "Advanced riders even work with teams of two or four. I saw a competition once with eight horses pulling old-fashioned coaches. It was something—but I didn't know how special it was until I had the chance to learn how tricky it can be driving just one horse!"

"You don't seem to be having any trouble with this," Stevie said.

Dinah smiled proudly. "It's not really hard at all," she said. "Want to try?"

Stevie did. In fact, she wanted to try very much, but she didn't want to take over when Dinah had just gotten her chance. She said as much.

"Don't worry about that," Dinah joked. "I'm not going to give you a *long* turn."

"Okay, then, I will," Stevie said. She took the reins from Dinah and moved into the driver's seat.

It took a few seconds to get used to the feel of the reins. Stevie was accustomed to holding reins as she sat in a saddle, but they were short ones, only a few feet long. This was different. These reins were more than ten feet long. They were much heavier in her hands and, she realized, would also be harder on the horse's mouth. Just a little pressure would signal the horse clearly. She tested her theory. She tugged almost imperceptibly on the left rein. Willingly the horse moved to the left.

"It works!" she said proudly.

"Sure it does," Betsy said quickly. "Now move back over to the right before we slide off the trail altogether."

Stevie looked to see what she'd done. The trail was rutted on either side for cars, trucks, or horse-drawn wagons. They were now perched with the right runner on the hump and the left almost off the edge of the trail.

Hastily Stevie reversed her gentle tugging, and the sleigh shifted easily back into the ruts on either side of the road.

"I think it's your turn now," Stevie said, returning the reins to Dinah's hands.

Dinah took over. Her eyes scanned the roadway in front of them, but they also scanned the forest around them. Stevie knew she was thinking about the two empty buckets in the back of the sleigh. Stevie scanned along with her.

"There's one!" Dinah declared, drawing the sleigh to a halt.

Betsy squinted. "I see it," she said, looking through the trees. She hopped down off the sleigh, grabbed the tools and a bucket, and was off, clambering through the snow, over some dried and frozen vines, to the maverick sugar maple tree. "If there's one here, there must be others," Betsy said reasonably. "Keep driving and looking!"

That made sense. Dinah flicked the reins. The horse began moving again. Stevie and Dinah paid little attention to the horse, who seemed to know what he was doing. All they cared about right then was finding another maple tree.

"There must be one, there must be one," Dinah said, nearly chanting.

"There it is!" Stevie declared, spotting the familiar and welcome painted maple leaf. The tree was off to the right, along a little pathway.

Without hesitation Dinah tugged at the right rein. Without hesitation the horse obeyed. Dinah flicked the reins to hurry him ahead. Again he obeyed.

"Let's get it!" Dinah said excitedly. The horse picked up the pace, sensing the urgency.

And then Stevie heard an awful sound—the protest of wood strained to its utmost. The shafts!

Dinah was so focused on the maple tree ahead, she almost didn't notice what was happening with the sleigh. She just gripped tightly at the reins.

Stevie didn't have time to take the reins from her. She merely grabbed the left rein and tugged. Instantly the horse responded, shifting back toward the left. Then he stopped abruptly. He wasn't aimed toward the maple tree then, but he also wasn't about to break the shafts or hurt himself.

"What did I do?" Dinah asked, surprised by their sudden stop.

"You were trying to turn too sharply," Stevie said. "It sounded to me like the shafts were about to crack."

"Oh, wow," Dinah said, as the realization came over her. "You're really some horsewoman, Stevie Lake. You don't even know how to drive this thing, and you saved me, and the horse, and the sleigh."

"Oh, I don't know," Stevie began to protest.

"Yes, you did," Dinah said. "I really almost blew it—just to tap one maple tree. It wasn't worth it—definitely."

"Who says we can't tap it now?" Stevie asked. She hopped down out of the sleigh, took the other drill and the last bucket and spile. In a few minutes she'd done the job and returned to the sleigh, now headed straight along the path toward the Sugar Hut.

While Stevie had been working on the last tree, Dinah told Betsy how Stevie's quick thinking had saved them from a disaster.

Betsy gave Stevie a hug. "Nice work!" Betsy said proudly.

"It's just because you're such a good teacher," Stevie said, a little embarrassed by all the attention her little rescue was getting.

"Whatever it is, I'm awfully glad you're here," Dinah said. Stevie was glad, too.

4

"TIME TO GET up!" Dinah announced the next morning at an hour that seemed very early to Stevie. She found that all the cold fresh air was very tiring. She could have slept for hours more.

"What's the hurry? Is it time to go collect the sap?" she asked.

"Not yet," Dinah answered, laughing a little. "It's still too cold for that. We have to wait until the temperature's just right so the sap will run the best before we go collect it. Part of winning this competition is knowing when that is."

"Okay, so we don't collect sap today. What *do* we do?"

"Horseback riding," Dinah said. "Today is my regular riding class, and you're cordially invited to join us. I know you're a better rider than I am and than most of my classmates, but I think you'll have fun. I hope you will, anyway."

"Don't worry," Stevie assured her. "If horses are involved, I always have fun. Let's go."

The girls bounded out of bed, washed and dressed quickly, and headed for the stable, followed out of the house by warnings and admonitions from Mrs. Slattery.

". . . and make sure you follow Mr. Daviet's instructions. Remember, no cantering and no leaving the ring without an experienced rider. Also, make sure your hard hat is snapped tightly and . . ." She went on, but the girls weren't listening.

"She really doesn't like the fact that I ride horses and love it so much," Dinah explained once they were outside.

"I can understand that," Stevie said. "Lisa Atwood— she's new at Pine Hollow, so I don't think you know her—has the same problem with her parents. Her mother thinks she ought to be taking ballet and painting instead. To please her mother, she takes ballet and painting *and* horseback riding."

"It isn't that with my parents," Dinah said. "They wouldn't want me taking ballet, either. It's too dangerous, they'd say. They knew someone once who had a freak accident on a horse and got brain damaged or something. They're convinced the same thing's going to happen to me, unless they can spend hours before each class warning me to be careful. It's very boring, but I have to let them do it, or they won't let me ride at all."

"Then let them do it, I guess," Stevie agreed. She felt a little sorry for Dinah. Stevie's parents never seemed to worry about her riding, and they never made it hard for her. If she occasionally had arguments about schoolwork or visits with friends or sleepovers or dates with Phil, that was okay. At least she didn't have arguments about riding—not often anyway.

"It's down this road," Dinah said, leading the way off the main street and along a muddy dirt road near where they'd turned off for the Sugar Hut the day before.

The stable was around a bend in the road, next to a stand of sugar maples, all duly tapped by other teams in the class competition who had gotten there first. It was a long low building with room to house about twenty horses. There was also a separate barn, used to store equipment and grain. Like Pine Hollow, it was surrounded by paddocks, including a working ring for classes that had been set up with a few jumps at one end of it. Everything was painted barn red and was spotlessly clean.

"I like it," Stevie said automatically.

"You like any place where there are horses," Dinah reminded her.

"True," Stevie said. "And Sugarbush is included."

"Good," Dinah said. "Now that that's settled, let's go get a horse for—uh-oh."

"What's the matter?" Stevie asked.

"There's nobody here," Dinah said. "Usually before class the parking area is filled with cars and the place is loaded with other kids taking the class. I have the funny feeling something's up."

Something *was* up. The girls walked into the stable to find it filled with horses and empty of riders. Dinah wanted to find somebody to ask what was going on, but she wasn't in so much of a hurry that she couldn't stop and introduce Stevie to Goldie.

Goldie lifted his head up over the door of his stall in greeting.

He was beautiful. He was a golden palomino gelding, and though Stevie had always had a soft spot for palominos, it wasn't his looks that made him so beautiful, it was his gentle manner and the spark of curiosity in his eyes.

"Oh," Stevie said, patting the horse and rubbing his cheek just the way Topside, the horse she usually rode, liked to be patted. Goldie snuggled Stevie's shoulder.

"Now I understand what this is all about," Stevie said. "We've just got to win the competition."

"What are you doing here?" a voice came out of one of the stalls.

Stevie and Dinah turned to look. It was Jodi Hale, Betsy's sister and Sugarbush's stable hand.

"I came for class," Dinah said.

"Canceled," Jodi said. "Don't you remember?"

Dinah flushed red with embarrassment. "No, why?"

"Because of the sugaring off," Jodi said. "Notices were posted everywhere for the last couple of weeks. How could you miss them?"

Dinah blushed. "I guess I just did. I'm sorry."

Stevie could tell that Dinah felt very uncomfortable. It was particularly embarrassing for her to have made a silly mistake in front of both Jodi, whom she admired a lot, and Stevie, her guest. Stevie wanted to make it easier for her. After all, anybody could make a mistake like that.

"I'm Stevie Lake," she said, introducing herself to Jodi. "I've heard an awful lot about you from Dinah."

"And I heard a lot about you from Betsy last night. You're the girl who figured out how to drive a sleigh before you'd even had one lesson, aren't you? It sounded like you really saved Betsy from making that goof, huh?"

That wasn't the subject Stevie wanted to have Jodi turn to. She was trying to make Dinah feel *better*, not more embarrassed. Stevie decided to try again.

"How come the classes are canceled?" she asked.

"It's because so many of the horses are used for sugaring, and most people are busy with that. Also, Mr.

Daviet has to spend the whole day at the Sugar Hut, so he can't teach."

"But Goldie's here," Dinah said. "Can we at least go for a trail ride?"

"You know the rules, Dinah, I'd have to go with you. You've got to have an experienced rider along on a trail ride."

"So you can take us. That would be fun. Besides, with you along we could go on the Rocky Road Trail—Mr. Daviet never takes the class on that one. It's supposed to be great. I can ride Goldie. Let's put Stevie on Evergreen—or do you want to ride Evergreen?—whatever you want is fine."

"Whoa there." Jodi held up her hand in a halting motion. "Who said I was going to go along? I've got Mark Carey coming over here in a half an hour for a stable lesson in tacking up."

There was a new sparkle in Dinah's eye. "Uh-huh. I just bet that's why he's coming over here. . . ."

Now it was Jodi's turn to look embarrassed. It was obvious that Mark was either Jodi's boyfriend, or somebody she wanted to be her boyfriend. Stevie's mind raced.

"Tacking-up lesson? Boy, I sure could use some pointers on that. If we can't ride, why don't Dinah and I just join in on that lesson? I forget," she continued

43

rapidly. "Which is it you put on first, the saddle or the bridle?"

Jodi gave Stevie a withering look. She knew she'd hit pay dirt. The last thing in the world that Jodi Hale wanted was to have two girls join in on her "lesson" with Mark Carey.

"And how do you keep the horse from biting your fingers when you put on the bridle?" Stevie pleaded.

"I just had a thought," Jodi said. "Although you need an experienced rider on the trail, it doesn't have to be *me*. From what Betsy said yesterday, Stevie here is a pretty experienced rider. You've done a lot of trail riding, haven't you?"

"Pretty much," Stevie said. "And not long ago I was on a five-day pack ride in the Rockies. Does that count? Of course, it was a dull trip, unless you want to consider the forest fire we had to get away from." She scratched her chin thoughtfully. "I guess I'd have to say I am pretty experienced."

"Well, then, why don't you two go out alone?" Jodi suggested.

"On the Rocky Road Trail?" Betsy pleaded.

"*Anything!*" Jodi said, obviously more than a little frustrated with Stevie and Dinah. That was exactly what Stevie had had in mind.

"I'll take Goldie, and Stevie can ride Evergreen?" Dinah asked.

"Yes," Jodi said.

"Then let's tack up," Stevie said. She didn't want to give Jodi time to change her mind.

"Good idea," Jodi said, showing no signs of changing her mind. She really wanted Stevie and Dinah out of there before Mark arrived. "Saddle first," she added wryly, letting Stevie know that she knew that Stevie knew perfectly well how to tack up a horse.

Stevie winked at her. Then she saluted, just the way Carole had taught her. "Aye, aye, ma'am," she said.

"I'll show you the tack room," Dinah said. They were off.

5

JUST AS THE girls were about to ride out of the paddock and into the forest, Jodi emerged from the stable with a worried look on her face. She seemed to be having second thoughts.

"Hey, please be careful," she said. "I mean, I know you're a pretty good rider, Dinah, and Betsy tells me Stevie's really experienced, but don't do anything silly, okay?"

"Okay," Dinah agreed. "You don't have to worry about us. We won't get hurt."

"It's not just that," Jodi told them. "It's also that Mr. Daviet would kill me if he knew I'd let you go out alone. The trail has been closed for the winter, and Mr. Daviet doesn't want anybody on it until he has a chance to check it out later in the week. It can be slippery in this kind of weather. Be careful and keep your mouths shut."

"We won't tell—ever," Dinah said.

"I promise," Stevie added.

"Thanks," Jodi told them. Then there was the sound of a car pulling into the stable driveway. Jodi disappeared as quickly as she'd appeared.

"I guess her 'student' is here," Stevie said, smiling.

"So we'd better get out of here," Dinah agreed. They began walking on a well-worn trail into the woods. "We're no longer welcome, right?"

Stevie nodded and they began their ride. Stevie loved riding in the snowy forest. There wasn't usually much snow in Virginia, even in the coldest winters. In Vermont you could count on a lot, especially in this mountainous area. Snow made the world feel different, smell different, sound different. This wasn't new snow. It wasn't even very fozen snow. It was a time of year when it was freezing at night, but in the daytime it was above freezing, and warm enough for snow to melt.

"Perfect sugaring weather," Dinah had told her. "Just perfect."

The snow was heavy and grainy. Every step of the horses' hooves brought up dark black mud from under the snow. In some places, where the snow was particularly deep and wet, the horses had to labor to make each step, picking their feet up out of the moist blanket of snow.

There was a loud thumping sound. Evergreen jerked in surprise but didn't try to run.

"What was that?" Stevie asked.

"Just a clump of melting snow falling from a branch," Dinah told her. "You'll hear a lot of that at this time of year. The horses won't even notice it next time."

As if on cue, another clump of snow fell off a nearby branch. Evergreen didn't flinch.

"There's a turn up ahead," Dinah said, looking back at Stevie. "The path goes three different ways. The trail we usually take is to the right. That stays in the valley and is pretty but kind of boring. Since Jodi said we could go on the Rocky Road Trail, we'll go to the left. Is that okay with you?"

Stevie was surprised Dinah even thought she had to ask. "Of course it is," Stevie said. "I love steep trails. I love to ride on mountains. I love to ride in the woods. And I promise never to tell anybody—except maybe all my best friends at home."

"I'm sure our secret will be safe with them," Dinah said, taking the uphill trail to the left.

The trail *was* steep, reminding Stevie of the lesson she'd received the day before about Ver-*mont*. The woods were thick and didn't provide a view yet, but Stevie had the feeling that once they had ridden into an open field they'd be looking out across the mountainous countryside. The challenge was to get that far through the snow, which seemed to deepen with each step.

The girls chatted contentedly as they rode, Dinah in the lead, Stevie close behind. Since Dinah hadn't been in Willow Creek for almost two years, she was eager for news of her friends, and Stevie was always glad to talk. Dinah also wanted to hear about Max and everything that went on at Pine Hollow. There was plenty of catching up to do.

Evergreen and Goldie both seemed familiar with the area and walked up the rocky trail willingly, finding firm footing with each step. The most important thing Stevie had learned about riding on steep trails was the need to lean forward, almost parallel to the horse's neck, while it was climbing upward. The other thing was that once she'd told the horse where she wanted to go, she had to let the horse do the work and find his own way. He would be the best judge of a safe route. So she relaxed and let Evergreen do the walking. It worked nicely.

Ahead of Stevie another clump of snow fell off the trees, this time landing on Goldie. He didn't like it. He started bolting away. Dinah did just the right thing. She held the reins securely and put pressure on his belly with her legs. The movements said, "I'm in charge." Goldie reverted to a walk immediately, swishing his tail to rid himself of drips of melted snow the same way he did for flies in the summer.

Stevie found herself oddly relieved. It was as if, deep down, she hadn't really been confident that Dinah was a good enough rider for this trail. Now that she'd seen her in action, she was pretty sure she was good enough. Stevie relaxed.

They continued their conversation. Stevie was telling Dinah about Carole's horse.

"His name is Starlight," Stevie began. "He's a bay gelding with a white star on his face. He's pretty young and hasn't finished his training, so Carole works with him all the time. She's there almost every day. Of course, she loves it. She'll make him into a championship horse."

"And she's going to be a championship rider, too, I just know it."

"So do I," Stevie agreed. "One of these days we'll be watching her at Madison Square Garden, or in the Olympics."

"Probably both," Dinah said.

For a while the path continued just as it had been. Then Stevie sensed that it was changing. Most of the trees were evergreens, and there were fewer of them.

"Now we get a chance to show our stuff," Dinah said. "There's a big open area ahead. We can trot in it. We can even canter."

"On the frozen ground?" Stevie asked. Stevie loved to canter, loved the feel of the horse's fast gait, rocking across an open area. However, it was dangerous to ask the horse to canter when it was so cold that the ground was frozen. For one thing, it could damage the horse's hooves. For another, the horse couldn't get traction on frozen ground and was more likely to slip.

"Oh, right," Dinah said. "Okay, then, let's just try a trot."

They come through the woods and into the open area Dinah had promised. As Stevie had suspected, they also had a spectacular view. She halted Evergreen just to look.

"It's something, isn't it?" Dinah asked.

Stevie just nodded. It seemed that they were miles from anything that appeared to be civilization, completely surrounded by snow-covered mountains, which were themselves dotted sparsely by evergreens. The sky above was blue and clear, spanning the vast mountainous wilderness. For the first time Stevie felt alone, felt the presence of the wild, felt vulnerable.

"Let's go," Dinah said. "Goldie's ready for a little trotting, aren't you?"

Without waiting for an answer from Stevie, Dinah signaled Goldie to move. Soon the horse was trotting obediently, though he had more than a little difficulty managing it in the deep snow. Still, he did what he was told. Stevie got Evergreen walking and then trotting as well. It was an odd gait in the snow, slower than usual, yet somehow smoother than usual. Stevie had been prepared to post, but found that in the snow she could sit the trot better than she could post. Since the snow was deep and the ground was hard, she knew it was difficult for the horse to move quickly, and she thought it was an imposition to ask him to do it.

"Let's just walk," she called ahead to Dinah. Dinah slowed down, but when she glanced over her shoulder at Stevie, there was a frown on her face.

"It's too hard on the horses," Stevie explained.

"Aw, come on," Dinah said. "They can make it. They've been cooped up in the stable for so long. . . ."

"That's not a good reason to let them do something dangerous," Stevie countered. She was surprised at how much she sounded like Carole. She was also surprised at how much Dinah had sounded like Stevie!

"All right," Dinah relented. "We have to stop now anyhow. The trail goes back into the woods here."

She turned Goldie to the left, reentering the forest and heading straight around the mountain. Unlike the first part of the path, this was relatively level and open. Dinah explained that the path merely circled the top of the mountain here, rejoining the lower path at the other end of the field they'd just left.

Boom! came another sound of a clump of snow hitting the ground. It was followed by a cracking sound.

"What's that?" Stevie asked.

"That's the sound of the ice melting," Dinah explained. "See, up here you can get big icicles on things in the winter. Sometimes on tree branches, sometimes on rocks. As the weather warms, the water in the icicles expands—remember that lesson in science class?—and the ice can crack as it melts. You can get the big booming sounds when it freezes as well. The pond by our house sometimes makes that noise. It's weird."

It *was* weird, and Evergreen thought so, too. He began flinching with each loud noise in the forest. And every time Evergreen flinched, Goldie started. Stevie kept a tight rein on Evergreen. He seemed to appreciate it and ironically relaxed a little.

As they continued along the path, Dinah gave a sort of guided tour.

"I've never ridden this before," she said, "but I've walked it a lot. In the summer we sometimes have picnics up here. There is a great rock formation up the mountain, just ahead." She pointed, holding both her reins in one hand. "We climb on it in the summer, and it seems like we can see forever. We won't be able to see it under the snow, but I'll tell you when—"

Boom!

Then, as Stevie watched in horror, Goldie took off! Dinah had been holding his reins with only one hand when he fled, and he was jolting her around so with his awkward terrified gait that she couldn't even grip the reins with both hands. Her left hand grabbed for his mane. That steadied Dinah, but it didn't do anything to slow Goldie down.

Stevie didn't know what to do, but she knew that sitting there on Evergreen wasn't going to do her or Dinah any good.

"Hyaaa!" she said to her horse, signaling him into action. He understood instinctively. He began moving as fast as the snow would allow.

"Stevie!" Dinah yelled.

"I'm coming," Stevie yelled back. "Hold on!"

"I'm trying!" Dinah said.

Then, just when Stevie thought things couldn't get any worse, they did. Suddenly the woods were filled with the booming sound of cracking ice and melting clumps of snow, but there was something else, too. There was the sound of wood breaking, and rocks skittering and crashing against one another. Stevie's mind raced even faster than her horse galloped. There was only one thing it could be. There were rocks rolling down the hill! It had to be the rock formation Dinah had been talking about. It was like an avalanche, and Dinah was riding right into the most dangerous part of it!

"Stop him!" Stevie yelled as loud as she could to be heard over the sound of the tumbling rocks.

"I can't!" Dinah called back.

It couldn't be true, Stevie thought. This beautiful

place, these wonderful horses. How could there be such danger? How could—

Then, thirty yards in front of her, Goldie, now even more terrified by the fearful threat, reared. It was a sight Stevie would never forget. Small rocks tumbled down the mountainside through the snow, kicking up puffs of snow and mud. In the middle of it was Dinah clutching the horse's mane for her life, her fingers desperately twined through the thick pale hairs at Goldie's neck. The horse, seemingly oblivious to the fact that the worst place in the world for him was right where he was, stood majestically on both his rear legs, whinnied, and screamed in horror, his front legs trembling with fear. It was as if the whole scene were in slow motion—until the moment he landed. As soon as his forelegs touched the ground again, he took off.

Stevie knew full well how hard it was for the horses to move quickly in the snow, but Goldie didn't seem to be having any difficulty at all. And as he bolted off, Dinah flew from the saddle, landing right in the path of the oncoming rocks!

"Help!" she cried, rolling over in the snow to protect her face. She also managed to crawl over toward a boulder to give herself some protection from the continuing shower of rocks.

There was nothing Stevie could do to help her. She

had to protect herself and Evergreen until the rocks passed, until it was safe for Dinah to get up—if she could. Stevie heard herself think those last three words and then shut them out of her mind. But her thoughts of the isolation and wilderness kept haunting her. *What if?* she asked. She forced the question back and out of her thoughts.

Evergreen stood, frozen in fear. Stevie's eyes were riveted to her friend, now curled up in fright. The stones continued tumbling down the mountainside, only now there were larger ones as well. Then Stevie's worst suspicions were confirmed. This kind of rock shower had to have been caused by something big, and she could see it coming.

The big rock was about three feet in diameter; it lumbered slowly but relentlessly down the hill, following the path of the smaller rocks before it, heading straight for Dinah!

"Move!" Stevie shrieked.

Dinah moved as she had never moved before. She shot out from behind the rock, dashing for safety.

"Faster!" Stevie yelled.

The boulder bounded downward, picking up speed, narrowing the distance, shifting now slightly to the left, then slightly to the right. Evergreen backed away. Stevie halted him. She had to stay by her friend.

"Help!" Dinah called.

"Here! This way!" Stevie called back. It was the only help she could give.

Dinah pulled herself through the snow, apparently unable to stand up. The boulder came closer. Dinah was moving, but she wasn't moving fast enough. Suddenly Stevie knew what she had to do. She kicked Evergreen and he courageously bolted forward, quickly moving into a lumbering canter. Stevie and Evergreen headed straight for Dinah.

"Give me your hand!" Stevie cried out. Dinah looked at her, terrified

"Your hand!" Stevie repeated.

Numbly Dinah reached up, sticking her hand in the air. Stevie shifted both reins to her left hand and leaned over to the right. Closer and closer. Stevie strained, shifting Evergreen's direction ever so slightly with signals from her legs. The horse understood the urgency and responded instantly. There was Dinah, frozen in horror, with her hand reaching, reaching.

An inch more, that was all it would take. Stevie strained. At the last possible second, her hand met Dinah's, grasped it, pulled. Dinah nearly flew up out of the snow, propelling herself upward, pulled by Stevie's grip.

Dinah clung to Evergreen's saddle with one hand and to Stevie with the other. She somehow managed to haul herself up onto the horse's rear. That was when Stevie dared to look up the hill again.

The boulder struck a tree, ricocheted to its right, crossed the trail just behind Stevie, Evergreen, and Dinah, and lumbered menacingly downward, hitting the rock Dinah had used as her hiding place. It shattered chunks of Dinah's safe haven and then continued down the mountain until it entered the flat meadow below, where it rolled to harmless stop.

The woods were once again silent.

It was over and they were safe. Stevie let out her breath. The only other sound she heard was Evergreen's snort of relief and the soft whimpering sounds coming from Dinah. She was hurt.

Stevie helped Dinah off the back of the horse and secured Evergreen's reins to a bare branch. Dinah lay in the snow, crying hard.

"Where do you hurt?"

"Is it over?" Dinah asked.

Stevie nodded. "It's done, we're safe. Are you okay?"

"If it's over, I'm okay," she said. "At least I think so, though I did get hurt when Goldie threw me. Did he rear?" she asked.

"Yes, and you were magnificent. You looked like a swashbuckling cowboy—if there is such a thing. Anyway, you stayed on for the rear, but when he took off, so did you—in the opposite direction."

"You mean *down*!"

"Yes, down. He took off up the hill, beyond where I

saw any trouble from the rocks. He's probably safe. We'll find him."

Then, as if he'd heard them talking about him, Goldie appeared from behind a tree, looking more sheepish than anything else. He paused to munch on a tempting piece of moss that peeked through the snow.

"Now, about you," Stevie began. She offered Dinah a hand so she could get up. Dinah took it gladly, but as soon as she began to rise, she also began to wince.

"Oh!"

"Where does it hurt?"

"Everywhere," Dinah said, tears of pain forming in her eyes. Stevie helped her up the rest of the way and led her to a tree stump, where she could sit.

"Is something broken?" Stevie asked.

"No, I don't think so. It's just scratches and bruises, but a falling rock can give you a mighty bad bruise. I hate to tell you where it hurts the most." From the way Dinah was sitting awkwardly on the tree stump, she didn't have to tell Stevie where it hurt the most. It was already clear.

"You've got to see a doctor," Stevie said, recalling the times she had hurt herself riding.

"No way," Dinah said. She stood up and took a few uncomfortable steps, as if to prove that nothing was broken and she would be all right.

"Why not?" Stevie asked.

"Because we promised," Dinah said. "We promised Jodi."

"What difference does that make?" Stevie asked. "Some promises were made to be broken."

"Maybe, but not this one," Dinah told her. "This one isn't just for Jodi's sake. See, if we tell, Mr. Daviet will be furious. Not only will he be angry with Jodi, but he'll be furious with me, and with you. He might never let me ride again. Even if he *did* let me ride again, my parents wouldn't, so it's the same. The answer is no doctor. I'll be okay. I promise. Anyway, we can take care of this. After all, if we can manage to avoid being killed by a landslide avalanche thing in the middle of the Vermont wilderness, we can certainly take care of a couple of cuts and bruises, can't we?"

Part of Stevie's common sense told her that it was foolish not to tell and get Dinah to a doctor, just to be sure. Another part of it told her that Dinah was up and walking, and there was no way a bruise where she sat was going to be fatal. And besides, Stevie knew first aid and she was pretty sure that Dinah was basically okay. After all, she *could* move and talk. She was going to be all right. Even more than all that, Dinah was definitely right about what would happen to Jodi and what Mr. Daviet would say and how her parents would react. She didn't like to think of Jodi losing her job, but the worst thing in the world would be if Dinah couldn't ride anymore. That was not a risk worth taking. Somehow they'd figure out how to take care of Dinah and keep the secret. Stevie was good at this kind of thing. She knew how to be sneaky for a good cause, and this was about as good as causes could get.

"Okay," Stevie agreed, confident now that they would succeed. "The promise holds. We'll take care of this ourselves and keep it to ourselves."

"Forever," Dinah said.

"Forever," Stevie promised.

"Which is just about how long it's going to take me to walk down this mountain," Dinah joked. "I mean, there's no way I'm actually going to *sit* in a saddle!"

It seemed to Stevie that this was a good time to make an exception to the "Get right back into the saddle" rule of falling off a horse.

"I'll ride Evergreen and lead Goldie," Stevie offered.

"Thanks, pal," Dinah said.

They began the long and slow journey home.

6

"HELLO, PHIL?" LISA said into the phone. She felt a little nervous about calling a boy, especially her best friend's boyfriend. Carole stood next to her and encouraged her with a smile. They were at Pine Hollow, doing just what Stevie had asked them to do. They were calling Phil to let him know Stevie was away and couldn't come to his pony club meeting.

"Yes?" Phil answered.

"This is Lisa Atwood, you know, Stevie's friend from Pine Hollow."

"Lisa, I know who you are," Phil said. "What's up? Is something wrong with Stevie?"

"Oh, no, she's fine," Lisa assured him. "At least we think she is, but you know Stevie, wherever she is, there's

62

trouble. Anyway, that's not why we're calling, but I guess it really sort of is. . . ."

Carole took the phone from Lisa's hand. She could do this better than that. "Hi, Phil, it's Carole here," she began. "Stevie has a friend in Vermont who invited her to something called sugaring off. . . ."

Very quickly Carole explained to Phil why Stevie wasn't going to be at his pony club meeting.

"Oh, no," he said, obviously disappointed.

"She tried to reach you before she left, but you were on that class trip," Carole reminded him. "That's why she asked us to call you when we knew you would be back."

"Thanks for calling," he said.

Carole could hear the sadness in his voice. She wanted to comfort him. "How's your riding coming?" she asked.

"Oh, very well," he said, brightening up. "Some of us went to a horse show on the class trip, and I watched some fancy riding. I think I picked up a couple of techniques. I can't wait to try them out. I'll be riding tomorrow."

Now he was talking Carole's language.

"What sort of techniques?" she asked eagerly.

"I was watching a hunter jumper class," he began. "And for the first time, I began to see the connection between the event that takes place in the ring and the actual hunt. In the ring there's a steady, even pace, and the *style* of successful jumping is emphasized. In the field, when you have the specific goal of having to trap a fox, it's important for you to have these skills."

"I used to ride a great hunter jumper," Carole said. "It was a wonderful feeling to complete the course on her. Starlight's great, but he's not disciplined enough for that kind of class in a show. He's much more interested in flashy high jumps, and he's so good at them—"

"I've seen you jump him," Phil reminded her. "He's a very special horse. He'll be doing championship jumping one of these days."

"I think so, too," Carole said. "The thing is that I believe I can train him so he can do both types of jumps."

"Well, that's what I meant about the techniques I was studying," Phil said.

Carole was never more comfortable than when she was talking about horses, and Phil was easy to talk to. They chatted, swapping hints and hunches, for more than ten minutes.

"Hey, I've got an idea," Phil said. "Since Stevie can't come to my pony club meeting, why don't *you* come to it? Can you get your father to bring you over?"

"Me?" Carole asked, suddenly uncomfortable again. "And what about Lisa?"

"Oh, sure, Lisa, too," Phil said. "It's an open unmounted meeting. Anybody can come. I'd be glad to have both of you there—especially you, Carole. We can talk more about jumping."

"We'll have to check with our parents," Carole said. "But it should be okay. I'll call if there's a problem."

"Great, see you then," he said.

"Okay, bye."

They hung up.

"What was that all about?" Lisa asked.

"We're invited to Phil's pony club meeting instead of Stevie."

"We are?" Lisa was more than a little surprised. "Carole, Phil is *Stevie's* boyfriend. What's she going to think?"

Carole got an uncomfortable sinking feeling. "Oh," she said. "I hadn't thought of that. I mean, it's the farthest thing from my mind. Stevie wouldn't think we were trying to steal her boyfriend. She even *asked* us to call him!"

"But she didn't ask us to go in her place," Lisa reminded her.

"But it's just a pony club meeting," Carole said. "Besides, he seemed so disappointed when Stevie couldn't be there, and so happy again when I said we could. There can't be anything wrong with that, can there?"

"Of course there can be," Lisa said. "What it comes down to is that he's Stevie's boyfriend, and it's not up to us to decide whether we can spend time with him when Stevie's out of town."

"But there will be two of us," Carole protested.

"Twice as bad," Lisa said.

"Girls, can you help me bring Nickel in from the paddock?" It was Mrs. Reg. That was Max's mother. She was the stable manager and a sort of part-time mother to the riders and their horses when she thought they needed it. She was also somebody who hated to see idle hands. Two girls standing together and talking qualified as four idle hands. Not surprisingly, Mrs. Reg had a way to put those hands to work.

"I'd get him myself," she said, "but he always runs from me." The three of them walked through the side door of the stable toward the paddock, where the frisky pony was gamboling around in the early spring morning. "He doesn't run from anybody else," Mrs. Reg went on, musing out loud. "He just runs from me. I never saw anything like it."

The two girls walked toward the pony. Mrs. Reg held back so as not to frighten him away. It was true that Nickel was scared of her. She'd never done anything to hurt him, so there had to be something about her that reminded him of something that *had* hurt him. Almost every horse had at least one thing that frightened him, and it was just about impossible to break those habits.

Lisa clicked a lead rope onto Nickel's halter and led him back toward the stable. When they reached Mrs.

Reg, the girls found she was still talking about Nickel's strange fear.

"Never saw anything like it—oh, yes, I did," she said. "I remember a mare we boarded here once who was afraid of me. She had strong likes and dislikes, that one. It seemed like she only ever liked one person at a time. She was devoted to the man who owned her and gave everybody else a hard time. She was beautiful, and I always wanted her to like me. I asked Max—my husband, your Max's father—to let me take care of her when her owner wasn't around, but Max wouldn't let me because she was so unpredictable. Then one day her owner went away. His mother was sick, and he had to stay with her for a couple of months. We didn't have any extra stable hands to take care of one more horse, so Max finally gave in. I got to look after the mare."

"Did she hurt you?" Lisa asked. Immediately she was sorry she'd asked the question. When Mrs. Reg was telling one of her stories—and she seemed to have thousands of them—she wanted to tell it her way without interruptions. Mrs. Reg ignored the question.

"It took a long time for me to change the way the horse felt about me. After a couple of weeks, though, she'd let me into her stall and let me groom her. She really needed it by then, too! By the end of six weeks, we were becoming friends. By the end of two months, I could ride her. I rode her every day then, and she was just as great to ride as I'd always known she would be." Mrs. Reg stopped. She had a habit of stopping stories just when they were getting really interesting.

"What happened when the owner came back?" Carole asked.

"Why, she gave him a hard time, of course," Mrs. Reg said. "Now you two stop all this jabbering and get Nickel back into his stall. Then, if you want to make yourselves useful, there are two stalls that need mucking out, and after that . . ."

The girls hurried away. If they stood there long enough, Mrs. Reg would load them down with enough work to keep them busy until midnight!

BY THE TIME Stevie and Dinah approached Sugarbush
Stables, Dinah had figured out that she could actually
ride, sort of. What she did was stand in the stirrups. She
wasn't very comfortable, and she knew she had a lot of
scratches and bruises nobody could see under her clothes
that she had to do something about, but both she and
Stevie were convinced they could get past the gimlet eyes
of Mr. Daviet and the Slatterys.

They weren't good enough to get past Jodi's eyes, however.

"Oh, no!" she said as they approached the barn.

"Don't worry," Stevie assured her. "We're still not telling. Dinah took a little spill. She's going to be fine. All

she has is a couple of scratches and bruises. No problem we can't handle all by ourselves."

The look on Jodi's face was clear relief.

"Thanks," she said. She didn't seem to want to hear any more about it, so Stevie and Dinah didn't bother to tell her how it had happened. "Look," Jodi said. "I'll take care of the horses for you now. I guess it's the least I could do. My sister came by earlier and said she was going to be collecting sap. She's expecting you two to meet her at the Sugar Hut. You go on up and get to work on that. But remember the promise—you can't tell her, either."

"We remember, Jodi," Stevie said, helping Dinah down out of the saddle. "Are you up for collecting sap now?" Stevie asked. The pained look on Dinah's face was answer enough.

"But it's got to be done," Dinah said. "Why don't you go over to the Sugar Hut and work with Betsy. I'll go home and take a long soaking bath."

"Won't your mother think that's suspicious?" Stevie asked.

"Not at all," Dinah assured her. "Even when I'm feeling fine, I like to soak in the tub. My mother won't suspect a thing."

"Are you going to be okay walking home?" Stevie asked.

"If I could just 'ride' a horse down a mountain, you bet

I can walk home. Trust me," she said. "This is a piece of cake."

Dinah waved bravely and walked, unsteadily, down the drive of the stable.

"The Sugar Hut is that way," Jodi said, pointing along another path into the woods. "About a quarter of a mile. You can't miss it."

"I know where the Sugar Hut is," Stevie said. "But thanks, anyway."

STEVIE LOVED COLLECTING sap with Betsy, though she didn't like the fact that she had to tell her a cover-up story about Dinah. She said Dinah had an upset stomach. Betsy was disappointed, but they had work to do. Once again, they had a horse-drawn sleigh, but this time it was a specially fitted flatbed sleigh with an enormous tank on the back of it. The two of them followed the same trail they had used to put out the buckets. As quickly as they could, they returned to each of their buckets, poured the nearly clear fluid that seemed to have miraculously appeared in the buckets into the tank, reset the buckets, and moved on.

Betsy seemed very pleased by the amount of sap they were getting. Stevie told her it was probably because the holes were so well drilled by the novice on the team.

At the end of their rounds, they returned to the Sugar

Hut, where Mr. Daviet siphoned the sap out of the tank and measured it and filtered it before storing it in one of the large tanks outside the Sugar Hut.

"Nice work," he said, looking at the numbers. "We're going to begin boiling tonight. Be sure to be here to help," he said. "That means Dinah, too. Uh, where is she?"

"She's home," Stevie said quickly. She wasn't sure if Mr. Daviet could know that she and Dinah had been at the stable. She decided to duck the question altogether. "She wasn't feeling very good this morning. Something about an upset stomach."

"Well, she'd better be here tonight," he said. "If the teams don't participate in all the activities, they can't get credit."

"I'll tell her, Mr. Daviet," Stevie said. "I'm sure she'll be feeling better by then."

"Probably will," he said. "I think there are some miracle cures going on around here. After all, it seems that your leg has gotten a lot better, too."

"Fresh country air," Stevie said with conviction. "Best medicine there is." She made a little jump, as if to assure him that she was, in fact, a lot better. He nodded noncommittally. Betsy stifled a laugh.

In a few more minutes, they were all done. Stevie was ready to go back to the Slatterys, and Betsy was headed for her house in the opposite direction. A half an hour later, Stevie was at the Slatterys', up in Dinah's bedroom, sharing the days' events.

"I tasted the sap," she said. "It was only slightly sweet. It's hard to imagine that that's going to become the wonderful stuff I like to put on pancakes.'"

"Do I really have to go tonight?" Dinah asked. She seemed totally unaware of anything Stevie had said after the part about Mr. Daviet's insistence that she be at the Sugar Hut tonight.

"He said so," Stevie said. "He sounded like he meant it. Can't you make it?" That was when Stevie realized that Dinah was in her bed and hadn't been out of it since she'd gotten home.

"I don't know," Dinah said. "I hurt an awful lot. And even if I do make it, I don't know how I'll hide all my injuries from my parents and Mr. Daviet. I mean, look at this bruise on my cheek!"

Stevie turned the light around so it pointed at Dinah. Then she saw. Dinah had several bruises, and a deep red scratch on one of her arms. The other was sore, but not bruised yet. On her right cheek, near her ear, there was an abrasion that was red now and would most certainly be black-and-blue by morning, if not before.

"I look like some kind of awful 'Before' picture," Dinah complained. "I've told my parents I had a stomachache."

"Same thing I told Mr. Daviet."

"That's all fine and good, but it's made my mother say I

shouldn't have anything to eat, and the fact is, the only part of me that's really working is my stomach!"

"Okay, okay, one problem at a time," Stevie said. "I told you in the first place that we could cope with this, and I meant it. First, we're going to do a makeover."

"Makeover! What do you think this is, a slumber party?"

"Not exactly," Stevie said. "The thing is, see, as every parent knows, when two girls get together, one of them is going to *try* to make the other one look better. Basically, as far as I can tell, that means that one of them wants to do an experiment on the other that they'd never *dare* do on themselves. Anyway, what you need right now is a new hairstyle—"

"What I need right now is *lunch*!"

"—that covers that ugly scrape on your face. And it's time you traded your usual stylish, tailored look of dress for the baggy, cover-up look."

"Oh," Dinah said, getting Stevie's drift. "You mean, with a little bit of help from my friend, I can actually go to the Sugar Hut tonight?"

"A promise is a promise," Stevie reminded her. "Now, sit up. We have work to do. And in the meantime, you may want this." Stevie fished into her pocket and brought out a mangled peanut butter sandwich. Dinah devoured it—not even wanting to ask what Stevie had done to acquire it.

Stevie went into the bathroom and loaded herself down with as much as she could carry. She had everything from mousse to electric curling iron, to makeup, to ribbons, to hair spray. When she returned, Dinah was still in the process of sitting up, wincing painfully. That, Stevie realized, would be the hardest thing of all to cover up. Pain was harder to mask than scratches.

"THAT'S WHAT YOU'RE wearing?" Mr. Slattery asked when Dinah and Stevie descended the stairs in time for supper.

"Isn't it cool?" Dinah asked with conviction. "Stevie did it!"

Both the Slatterys looked at Stevie, apparently seeing her in a new light. Stevie had the feeling she might not be so welcome in their house another time. However, there was an appearance to keep up.

"It's a new look we've been using in Virginia," Stevie said. "It's all the rage."

The Slatterys looked back at their daughter. Her clothes were loose-fitting, even baggy, but the truly unusual aspect of her was her coiffure. It had taken Stevie hours. Most of Dinah's hair was piled on top of her head. On the right side, however, there was a hand-sized curl that swept across her right eye, obviously obscuring her vision, downward below the chin line, and then back up, fastened behind her ear. It was held in place with a large

75

bow, and about half a can of hairspray that had been sprayed on top of a lot of mousse.

"I bet it is the rage," Mr. Slattery said.

"At least I bet it makes all your parents in a rage," Mrs. Slattery added.

"It makes me feel like I only have half a daughter," Mr. Slattery said. "Just the left half. The rest of her is in some kind of cocoon. Oh, no, that's not a cocoon. That's my sweater! Isn't it a little large for you?"

"I'm hungry," Dinah said, trying to change the subject. It worked. Her mother was so pleased to know that her stomach was feeling better that all talk of her outlandish outfit stopped while dinner was served.

STEVIE COULD SMELL the Sugar Hut before she could see it. She and the Slatterys drove over to Sugarbush and walked the short walk into the woods to the Sugar Hut.

"Oh, if only I could smell some pancakes, too!" Stevie declared. "I could smell to my heart's content and never put on a pound!"

"It's really something, isn't it?" Dinah asked, smiling at Stevie's reaction. "Once they start the actual evaporation process, the whole area smells of maple syrup and wood smoke. Sometimes I think it's the most wonderful scent in the world."

"For the first few hours," her mother reminded her. "Then we all start thinking that the thick syrupy smell will never end. It makes us thirsty, and we all crave salty foods to counterbalance all the sweetness in the air."

A small gust of wind brought the full impact of the evaporation process to Stevie then. She still thought it was wonderful. She hurried to the Sugar Hut to see it all for herself. Dinah followed, carefully.

Betsy greeted them outside the Sugar Hut.

"Dinah? Is that you under there? What happened to your hair?"

"Stevie did it. Isn't it cool?" she said quickly, allaying any impending insults.

Betsy glanced at Stevie and the look indicated she was promising herself never to let Stevie try a makeover on *her*. Stevie did the only thing she could under the circumstances. She beamed proudly.

"And, uh, how's your *stomach*?" Betsy asked.

"A little better," Dinah lied.

"Enough better to taste maple, I hope."

"Definitely," Dinah assured her. They proceeded into the Sugar Hut.

The main feature of the inside of the Sugar Hut was the large evaporation area, filled with pans of bubbling sap. Beneath the pans a wood fire burned brightly, stoked from time to time by some of Dinah's riding classmates. Others stood at the edge of the tank, skimming off white bubbles as they formed on top of the syrup. All around, people from town, mostly parents of the students, stood and chatted. Stevie found they had endless thoughts about comparisons of this year's sap and syrup versus last year's or the year before.

"I think the syrup is going to be a lighter color now, because the season came so early this year," one man said.

"We tapped the trees the same time last year," another said. "And that syrup was amber."

"Not really. It was darker than amber," somebody else said.

"Not compared to the year before that," added another parent.

Stevie was mystified by it all. All that seemed to matter was that very soon the first batches of maple syrup would be coming out at the far end of the evaporation area.

"Almost ready!" Mr. Daviet announced. He stood poised with a bucket and a filter made of cotton flannel to remove any remaining impurities, waiting for the first drops of the final product.

"Go get some snow!" he instructed a few riders. Obediently three boys grabbed trays and ran out into the night. In a few minutes they returned, announcing that the snow was ready and waiting outside. Mr. Daviet nodded acknowledgment, but his full attention was really on the pan in front of him.

He studied some instruments. Stevie didn't know for

sure what they were, but one of them appeared to be a thermometer.

"When it's finished, real maple syrup boils at a different temperature from the sap," Dinah explained. "Mr. Daviet studies all his instruments, but the true sugar maven swears that he just 'knows' when it's ready."

Parents and students gathered around Mr. Daviet, waiting, watching. All conversation stopped. Stevie could feel the tension in the air.

Mr. Daviet leaned forward and sniffed. He smiled. He used a wooden spoon and stirred, lifting a spoonful of the sweet liquid into the air and then pouring it. He studied the flow, the color, the weight by his own measure. He mixed a few seconds more. Nobody said a word.

Finally he checked the thermometer again, looked at two other measuring instruments, did the spoon swishing and pouring, studied more closely.

"Syrup!" he announced proudly. With that, he opened the spigot at the far end of the pan and let the sweet light brown liquid flow through a filter and into the shiny clean bucket he held nearby. As soon as the first bucket was filled, he began filling a second. When the whole pan had been emptied, several students were charged with the job of cleaning it so it could be filled again and the whole process could start over.

Other students had what appeared to Stevie to be an even more important job. They took the first bucket of syrup, poured it into another pan on a smaller stove, and continued boiling it.

"What's the matter with it?" Stevie asked.

"Nothing," Dinah said. "But the first bucket is always used for Sugar-on-Snow. For that, it needs just a little more boiling. It's about our turn to do some work. Do you want to try it?"

"Sure," Stevie agreed. She found herself standing at a small wood stove, stirring maple syrup that bubbled. It didn't take long and it wasn't very hard work. Within a few minutes it was obviously thicker and darker than syrup. It was foamy and, if possible, even sweeter.

"It's ready!" Dinah announced.

A few kids came to the stove to help. Most of them ran outside. Stevie wasn't sure why they did that, but she was pretty sure it had to do with the trays of snow.

Stevie and two boys carried the pan outside to the trays of snow. Other kids took ladles and began dribbling the thick mass directly onto the clean snow. Almost instantly the snow cooled it into chewy maple-flavored twists and strings.

Stevie took two pieces. One was for herself, and the other was for Dinah, who was standing cautiously by the door. Stevie hoped the candy would make her feel better.

"Oh," Stevie said, actually surprised by how wonderful it tasted. "After this, there's no point in eating another candy bar. Nothing that comes in a wrapper could possibly taste as good as this."

Very soon all the Sugar-on-Snow had been devoured, and everyone began to return to the Sugar Hut, where Jodi had laid out a whole tray of cider to drink.

As soon as they stepped inside, Stevie noticed that somebody had stoked the fire. The fact that there were about fifty people in there, compounded by the hot fire and the smoke and evaporating sap, made the Sugar Hut very warm. People began removing layers of clothing. Stevie took off her jacket and her sweater. She even rolled up the sleeves of her shirt. Dinah stood by the door, still swathed in her sweater and gloves. She even had her hat on.

Stevie took one look at Dinah's pained expression and knew what the problem was. Dinah couldn't afford to take anything off. If she even removed one layer of clothing, surely some of her cuts and bruises would be visible, and her parents would start asking questions.

Stevie to the rescue.

"How about a moonlight Frisbee game?" she proposed, locating a pie tin that had just been used to carry a load of snow for Sugar-on-Snow. The young riders in the crowd eagerly agreed. Pretty soon Stevie had a game organized.

All Stevie wanted was to get enough kids outside so

that Dinah could disappear in the dark. She could sit somewhere quietly, and nobody would notice how odd she looked and how uncomfortable she was.

Betsy threw the pie plate to Stevie. It glinted in the moonlight and caught the stream of light that came from the windows of the Sugar Hut. Stevie made a dash for it. She almost caught it, when she ran smack into Jodi, who was headed toward the Sugar Hut from the woods beyond. The two of them ended up in the snow together.

Stevie laughed at the ridiculous situation. But the older girl just stood up and brushed off the snow. Then, without a word, she marched toward the trail that led to the stable. Stevie wouldn't have minded if Jodi had said hello, but Jodi seemed very angry and in a big rush.

Stevie retrieved the fallen pie plate, tossed it back to Betsy, and decided to explore where Jodi had come from. She wanted to know what had gotten Jodi riled up. It wasn't hard to follow her footsteps back into the woods. It got easier when she heard the whimpering sound.

There was Dinah, perched uncomfortably on a snow-covered rock, crying her heart out.

Suddenly Stevie was filled with doubt. If Dinah hurt so badly, then maybe she ought to see a doctor. Maybe something really was wrong. She shared her thoughts.

"No," Dinah said. "I don't hurt that badly. I'm okay."

"Then what are you crying about?" Stevie asked.

"Nothing," was all Dinah would say.

8

WHEN MORNING CAME, Stevie still felt worried about Dinah. She wasn't worried about her cuts and bruises so much. They were turning horrendous colors, and it was obvious that they hurt, but it was clear to Stevie that something else was hurting Dinah even more. What was worse, she wouldn't talk about it.

"What happened last night at the Sugar Hut?" Stevie asked.

"Oh, I just got hit on the head with a falling icicle," Dinah said.

"Come on, Dinah," Stevie said, persisting.

"It was nothing," Dinah insisted. "And I don't want to talk about it."

Stevie was irritated with her friend, and she looked at

her to tell her that without words. What she saw, however, made all her irritation disappear. Dinah was crying. Tears welled up in her eyes and splashed down on her cheeks.

"I think I just need to be alone," Dinah said. "Please?"

Stevie relented. Dinah just wasn't in the mood to talk. Stevie could understand that—sort of. Even with Lisa and Carole, there were times when they didn't want to talk—not many, though. Thinking about her friends made her wish they were there. They'd know what to do and how to take care of Dinah. And if they were here, maybe Phil could come, too. . . .

Stevie let her mind wander. Thoughts of Phil made her remember the Pony Club meeting that was coming up. She hoped her friends had remembered to call him. Of course they had, she assured herself. They were her *friends*. Friends helped one another, doing things like calling boyfriends and collecting sap. That thought brought Stevie back to the reality of Dinah's bedroom.

"How about collecting? We're supposed to go out with Betsy today. Are you up for it?"

Dinah shook her head. "Cover for me, will you?"

"Okay," Stevie said. She slipped into her clothes and went downstairs, leaving Dinah alone to sleep and heal. Not knowing what her friend was crying about bothered Stevie, but she knew there were times when you shouldn't push. This was one of them.

Mrs. Slattery laid out a big breakfast of pancakes and the last of last year's maple syrup for Stevie. Stevie explained that Dinah still wasn't feeling well and wanted to sleep in. A look of concern crossed Mrs. Slattery's face.

"It was a late night last night," Stevie reminded her. "And Dinah really played hard at the Frisbee game. She outplayed everybody there. No wonder she's tired!" Stevie put as much conviction into it as she dared.

"Funny," Mrs. Slattery said. "She's always sort of hated Frisbee games."

"She's changed, believe me," Stevie said.

"Hmmmm," Mrs. Slattery remarked.

Stevie decided to change the subject.

"Can I have more pancakes, and can you give me Betsy Hale's phone number?" Stevie asked. "And, I wonder, how is it that the maple syrup flows only at this time of year?"

The pancakes appeared on her plate. Betsy's phone number appeared on a piece of paper next to it. But best of all, Mrs. Slattery began telling Stevie all about maple sap.

"The tree is beginning its growth season, and it needs sap to carry nutrients to the areas of the tree that will grow the most when the warm weather comes. There will be leaves, too. . . ."

One thing Stevie had learned was that everybody in Vermont loved to tell anybody who didn't happen to come from Vermont all about the sugaring season. Mrs. Slattery was soon much too busy discussing nutrients even to think about her daughter's mysterious ailment. That was just what Stevie had counted on.

Once Stevie had filled herself with all the pancakes she could eat, and listened to all the maple lore she could stand, she excused herself and called Betsy.

Betsy was disappointed to learn that Dinah wasn't feeling well. Stevie wanted to tell her what was really wrong, but she had promised Dinah nobody would ever know. Even though she didn't like keeping a secret from Betsy, it was better than breaking a promise to Dinah.

"I noticed she wasn't looking like she felt great last night," Betsy said. "It didn't have anything to do with the makeover, did it?"

"I don't think so," Stevie assured her. "In fact, it seemed to make her feel better. She thought she was well enough to go out, but it turned out she really wasn't. Anyway, it's you and me again today for sap collecting. Are we a team, or what?"

"What?" Betsy joked. "No, really, we're a team. And not just at sap collection."

"How's that?" Stevie asked. She detected a note of excitement in Betsy's voice. Something was up.

"Well, after we collect, my father said he'd drive us over to the ski area two towns away. Want to come?"

"Wow!" Stevie said. "It would be great! I can see me

now, *schussss*ing down a mountainside, just like one of those Olympic skiers. I can't wait!"

Something in Stevie's eagerness gave her away.

"You've never skied before, have you?" Betsy asked.

"No, but it sure looks like something I could pick up quickly."

Betsy laughed. "Either that, or else I'll end up picking you up quickly! Anyway, it is fun, and it'll be fun to teach you. Jodi's working today. You can use her skis. What size shoe do you wear?"

It took another ten minutes on the phone to settle on whose equipment Stevie could borrow, and it took another few minutes after that to convince Mrs. Slattery that Stevie should go skiing. The Slatterys, it turned out, weren't just nervous about girls on horseback. They were nervous about girls on skis, too. Finally it was arranged. Stevie and Betsy would spend the morning in the woods and the afternoon on the slopes. As far as Stevie was concerned, that would make it just about a perfect day. The only sour note was that it would have been so much fun to share it all with Dinah, too.

9

STEVIE HAD ALWAYS thought of herself as a person who wasn't afraid of very much. She wasn't afraid of learning to ski. She wasn't afraid of going up on the lift. She wasn't afraid of getting off the fast-moving seat at the top of the hill. She wasn't afraid—until she turned around at the top of the mountain and looked down.

"That's where we came from?" she asked, pointing to what seemed to be a very distant ski lodge at the bottom of the hill.

"Yup," Betsy said, looking amused. "And that's where we're going, as well."

"How?" Stevie asked, gazing at the narrow strips of wood that were to serve as her transportation.

"*Schusssss!*" Betsy declared. "Now, here's how you put these things on."

While Stevie watched, in case she would ever live to do this again, Betsy slid the skis under her feet, lined them up with the oversized boots Stevie was already wearing, snapped a few things, and declared the job done.

"They won't come off?" Stevie asked.

"Not unless you want them to, or if you need them to," Betsy said. "See, they are designed to snap off if you start tugging on them at awkward angles. That's a signal to the ski that you're in trouble. If you've fallen and are tumbling, the last thing you want is to have skis attached to your boots, so they simply snap loose and you're free."

"To fall?"

"I wouldn't put it that way," Betsy said. "But I guess that's what it amounts to. Now, are you ready? This *is* the beginner slope. It may be a little tricky for you, but I'm sure you can do it."

Stevie took a pole in each hand and tried to lift her foot.

"Slide, don't li—" Betsy began, but it was too late. The tip of Stevie's ski had caught in a little clod of snow. As Stevie lost her balance, the other ski slid forward and she slid backward, onto her seat.

"Congratulations," Betsy said. "That's your first fall. Now you're a bona fide snow bunny."

She offered Stevie a hand and helped her back up. Before Stevie tried to move again, Betsy gave her a few pointers. She showed her how to walk, without lifting her toes.

Stevie tried again. This time she stayed upright. The skis made little pathways for themselves in the spring snow. When Stevie stopped walking, she even found that the skis continued sliding.

"I'm skiing!" Stevie declared. Betsy beamed because it was true.

They spent most of the next half hour stepping and sliding around at the top of the hill. Then Betsy said it was time to try some downhill skiing.

"Like the Olympians?" Stevie asked eagerly.

"No, like a beginning skier," Betsy replied sensibly. She then turned, as she had shown Stevie how to do it, and faced slightly downhill. "We'll make a zigzag pattern," she said. "That way you're never completely going downhill except, of course, when we turn from a zig to a zag."

Stevie thought she had the idea. Betsy led the way; Stevie followed. It took a lot of concentration, but Stevie found she could actually control her direction and her speed, just a little bit. Of course, there was the time she lost control and whizzed past Betsy, straight into another beginner. The two of them fell down together and laughed together. Then they tried to help one another up. It took Betsy's help to succeed.

Soon Stevie realized that falling down wasn't so bad. It usually meant sitting down more than anything else, and it also usually meant falling on the soft snow—except when Stevie toppled onto another skier, or one toppled onto her.

"Hey, I'm really getting the hang of this," she said, having worked her way back to a standing position all by herself. "I think that was my seventeenth fall. Does that mean I'm still just a snow bunny, or have I become something bigger, like maybe a snow elephant?"

Betsy didn't have time to answer the question before Stevie fell again. This time she announced "Eighteen!" on her way down.

As the afternoon wore on, Stevie fell less often and remained standing more often. She found that not only could she control the skis and her direction and her speed some of the time, she could even do it most of the time.

It took them more than an hour to get to the bottom of the hill the first time. The second time it was a mere twenty minutes.

"This is really great!" Stevie declared.

"I knew you'd love it, and I knew it wouldn't take you long to get the hang of it," Betsy said. "Anybody who is as fast a learner as you with horses is sure to be good on skis as well."

"Are they connected?" Stevie asked while she executed a near-perfect turn—meaning she didn't fall down or hit anybody *and* she ended up in the direction she wanted.

"No, it's just that you're smart and coordinated. Those things are important."

Stevie felt very proud of her accomplishment. Within the next hour she even found herself giving pointers to beginners she found floundering in the snow at her feet.

"Get up and try again," she urged one person. "It's really worth it once you get the hang of it."

"Come on, let me show you this little side path," Betsy said. "You're good enough now, and it is part of the beginners' trail."

Stevie followed obediently. At first she didn't see the trail at all. All she saw was a row of fir trees with their snow-covered branches hanging all the way to the ground. Betsy went straight up to one of the branches, lifted it up, and went under. Stevie did the same.

As soon as she went under the branch, it was as if she had entered a magical kingdom. Suddenly there was total silence. The blanket of snow on the branches made walls and a ceiling for a hideaway, muffling all the outside sounds. She and Betsy were standing in a naturally made cathedral.

Stevie was stunned. She was afraid to move. If she moved, it might shatter the dream and it would all disappear. Then she and Betsy would be back out on the noisy slope, surrounded by tumbling snow bunnies. "If I blink, will it go away?" she asked.

"It's something, isn't it?" Betsy answered. "Dinah and I discovered this last year when one of her skis broke off and slid under that tree. This beginners' slope is filled with people who have never been here before and probably will graduate to intermediate tomorrow. They never find it and they never come back. It's ours." Betsy began moving again, slowly. "Come on," she said. "We can sit on that rock over there. . . ."

Stevie followed, very carefully. All of her senses were alert. She felt the cool air on her face, and the smooth motion of her skis beneath her. The muffled silence surrounded her. The scent of fresh evergreen filled her.

Betsy looked over her shoulder at Stevie and laughed. "Don't worry," she said, "it will be here forever, at least until the snow melts. Then it just changes colors. Dinah and I walked up here last summer. It was different, but it was the same." She leaned over and unsnapped her skis. Then she helped Stevie do the same. They propped their skis and their poles against a tree trunk. Betsy led Stevie up onto a rock. She dusted snow off the crest of it and sat down, inviting Stevie to do the same.

"Dinah and I called this the palace throne," she said.

Stevie could see why. It was higher than anything else in the magical clearing and overlooked the whole kingdom. From there Stevie could even see a little stream, bubbling beneath layers of snow and ice.

"This is almost my favorite part of skiing," Betsy said. "Jodi likes to do downhill racing. My parents are cross-country buffs. Me? I like both kinds of skiing, but mostly I like the beauty of a place like this."

"So everybody in your family skis?" Stevie asked.

"Definitely," Betsy said. "Just about everybody in Vermont skis. It's a sort of unofficial state pastime."

"And horseback riding? Are you all riders as well?"

"I guess so. Jodi and I have been riding for a long time."

"She's really good, isn't she?" Stevie asked.

"Sort of," Betsy said. "Personally, I think she's more in love with the glamour of riding than she is with horses. She even wears her breeches to school sometimes. And you should have heard her boasting when she got the job at Sugarbush. She knows her stuff, but it's like she almost doesn't care."

Stevie thought about the Jodi that Dinah admired so much. It seemed hard to think that Dinah's Jodi was the same person Betsy was describing. How could somebody who didn't care about horses be so worried about Dinah and about keeping her job?

"Aren't you being a little hard on your sister?" Stevie asked.

Betsy shrugged.

Stevie picked up a handful of snow and automatically began shaping it into a snowball. She didn't intend to throw it, however. That wouldn't have felt right in this magical place. She merely tossed it from hand to hand. "What about your parents?" she asked. "Do they ride?"

"They're trying to become riders," Betsy answered. "One night at dinner last fall Dad announced that because Jodi and I were spending so much time at Sugarbush, he and Mom had figured that the only way they'd get to see us was if they started spending time there as well. They signed up for a bunch of classes and they ride regularly. Dad says he's going to take a jump class this summer. Isn't that neat?"

"Definitely," Stevie agreed. Stevie's feeling about horseback riding was that it was so much fun that nobody should miss out on it. She wouldn't have minded at all if her parents had decided to take it up—as long as they weren't in her class and didn't try to tag along on her fun with Carole and Lisa.

"Is your mother good, too?" Stevie asked.

"She mostly likes to go on trail rides. Fortunately there are zillions of trails through the woods here, so she doesn't get bored."

"Oh, I know there are," Stevie said.

"You do? How?" Betsy asked.

"Well, Dinah and I—" Stevie stopped short. Betsy didn't know about Dinah's accident. She also didn't know that Stevie and Dinah had been on a trail at the time. Nobody knew that. Nobody *could* know that. "—Dinah and I were talking about them last night. She told me there were zillions. I wish I could go on some of them, too."

"Too bad you can't," Betsy said. "That's the one drawback of the sugaring off. Mr Daviet won't let anybody ride on the trails. By the end of the week, he'll relent a little. He usually takes a couple of riders out on a trail ride or two, but don't count on it. For now, he's too busy at the Sugar Hut anyway."

Stevie sighed silently to herself. She'd come close to giving away the secret, but she hadn't. She didn't think Betsy even suspected.

Betsy told her they should be getting back. If they worked quickly, they'd have time for one more run on the mountain before they had to go home. Very carefully Stevie took the ball of snow she'd been shaping, formed it back into a flat piece of snow, and put it back approximately where she'd found it. It didn't look exactly undisturbed, but it was the best way Stevie had of leaving the magical cathedral close to the way she'd found it. She wanted to find it that way when she returned, and she promised herself she would, someday.

* * *

"SKIING IS WONDERFUL!" Stevie announced to Dinah when she returned to the Slatterys later that day. "Oh, I wish you could have been there. It was such fun!"

"Did Betsy show you the castle?"

Stevie grinned and nodded. "Is that what you call it? I couldn't decide between a castle and a cathedral."

"Well, the throne . . ."

They took some time to decide which it was. In the end they concluded that it was a cathedral in a castle that had thrones for the reigning royals. Even more important, they decided they would go together someday soon.

"Your mother told me you wouldn't eat anything. She's getting worried about your stomachache. But how *are* you doing?" Stevie asked, noting with some disappointment that Dinah was still in bed.

"More or less okay," she said. "Fortunately, I've managed to keep my mother from noticing my face, but everything really hurts."

"Let's take a look," Stevie said in her most matter-of-fact, mother-taking-charge tone of voice. Obediently Dinah swung her feet over the edge of the bed and sat upright. First Stevie checked the scrape on her face. It was definitely ugly, but it seemed to be healing. Then Dinah hiked up her pajama bottoms to display the damage on her legs. Stevie examined them, pretending that Dinah was a horse who needed some tending. Stevie was pretty good at tending to horses. She didn't have much experience with humans, but she figured they couldn't be terribly different. At least she hoped they weren't.

The long scrape on Dinah's leg was red, but less so than it had been. "The infection is going away," Stevie said. "See how the redness is paling. So keep putting the goo on it. The same goo should go on your face, too. It helps."

There was a deep purple bruise on one thigh that Dinah said hurt, but was okay. Stevie agreed. It was just a bruise. No swelling or anything. Then, on one of Dinah's knees Stevie found something that worried her a little. It was purplish and swollen. The bruise had the distinct shape of a horseshoe.

"I think I remember Goldie using that knee as a starting block for his hundred-meter dash," Dinah joked weakly. "It's hard to put weight on it."

Stevie wrinkled her brow and pursed her lips thoughtfully. "You need a leg wrap," she said finally.

Dinah laughed. "You think I'm some kind of a horse?"

"Not really," Stevie said. "But you know if you saw that kind of swelling on a horse, you'd wrap it, right?"

"I guess," Dinah agreed. "But you were always better at horse care than I was."

"So wouldn't that be right for a person, too?"

"Why not?" Dinah answered. "I think there's an elastic bandage in the bathroom. You do the honors."

Stevie felt comfortable doing this. Horses often needed to have their legs wrapped. Sometimes it was to help with healing. Other times it was to avoid injuries. In any case, one of the first things she'd learned to do for horses was to wrap legs. She did it quickly and efficiently.

"Makes me feel like having oats for supper," Dinah said. She giggled. Then she whinnied for emphasis. It was just about the first laugh Stevie had heard from her since her fall. It sounded very good to Stevie. She thought that maybe laughter would be better medicine even than leg wraps.

"No, hot mash," Stevie said. "We believe in it for our sick horses. Of course, the vet says it doesn't make a darn bit of difference to the horses, but it makes *us* feel better."

Then Stevie finished checking the other wounds. Like the first bad scratch and the bruise, they all appeared painful, but healing.

"Now it's time to walk you around the paddock a few times," Stevie said. "If you don't keep moving at least a little, you're going to stiffen up."

Dinah was afraid and Stevie could see it. She was afraid of how much it was going to hurt. Stevie didn't know what to do for a person who was afraid, but she knew what to do for a horse who was. The first thing any rider did with a frightened horse was to talk. Stevie helped Dinah stand up, and she began talking.

"I couldn't believe how high that beginners' hill was when we first got off the lift," she began, holding one of Dinah's arms across her shoulder and putting her own arm around her friend's waist. She helped her stand. "The lift ride had made it seem like nothing at all, but the first look down . . ."

Dinah took a few steps.

". . . then by the time I'd fallen down eighteen times, I seemed to be getting the hang of it—skiing, I mean, not falling down."

Dinah laughed and walked some more. Stevie let her walk more on her own.

"I've got to tell you, though, there are a lot of people out on that hill who really don't know what they're doing. They're just falling all over the place. One guy actually fell on me twice! Of course, I'd already fallen into the snow by the time he fell on me!"

Stevie could feel Dinah shaking. She looked at her in alarm. But Dinah was just shaking with laughter. She continued to walk around her own room, more confident with each step.

"Oh, I *do* wish I'd been there," she said.

"You will be next time," Stevie promised. And from the way Dinah was walking, Stevie was pretty sure she was right.

10

A FEW DAYS later Stevie found herself running up the stairs to Dinah's room.

"You've got to get up," she said. "All the while when your mother was giving me breakfast, she was talking about doctors. She also said something about Kaopectate and milk of magnesia. What I mean is you've *got* to get up."

Dinah sat bolt upright in bed, swung her feet around, and stood up without hesitating. She grimaced instead. "I can do it. I *will* do it."

"You're darn right you will. We can't have your mother taking you off to a doctor."

"No way."

Dinah got dressed. Slowly.

Stevie recreated her "makeover" look as she'd done each day since the accident.

"This hairdo is really something," Dinah said, giggling, as she examined Stevie's handiwork in the mirror over her bureau. "Do you think it will become fashionable sometime, someplace?"

"Wherever and whenever that is, I hope I'm not there," Stevie said. Dinah agreed.

"Is something wrong?" Betsy asked.

The big flat sleigh with the collecting vat had just jolted to an awkward halt. Dinah was wincing in pain from the amount of pulling she'd had to do on the reins to get the horse to stop.

"No," she said quickly. "I'm just not as good at this as you are."

"Then let me do it," Betsy persisted. She'd been trying to get Stevie and Dinah to let her take the reins since they'd started. The one thing Dinah and Stevie had agreed on before they'd gotten to the Sugar Hut that morning was that Dinah would have to be the driver. There was no way she could walk in the snow and collect sap. She still hurt too much.

"No, I'm fine," Dinah assured her. "I've just got to learn to do this right."

"That's for sure," Betsy said a little unkindly.

"There are some more of our buckets!" Stevie said,

attempting to change the subject. Dinah got the horse moving and drew up near the next grove of their sugar maples.

Stevie and Betsy hopped down off the sleigh and headed for the buckets. It took only a few minutes to empty the buckets into the vat. It took only a few more minutes to remove the spiles from the tree trunks. Sugaring time was coming to an end, and all the riders had been instructed to remove their equipment, too. All the buckets and spiles were loaded onto the back of the sleigh, and they went off in search of another grove with their buckets on the trees.

The sleigh went over a bump in the road.

"Ouch!" Dinah said.

"What's the matter?" Betsy asked automatically.

"Nothing," Stevie and Dinah answered in unison. Keeping a secret from Betsy was turning out to be a very hard thing to do. This time it was Dinah who attempted to change the subject.

"How are your parents coming with their riding lessons?"

"Oh, great," Betsy said. "In fact, they're going on a trail ride this morning."

"They are? I thought Mr. Daviet said nobody would go out on any of the trails until after sugaring off was over."

"He did," Betsy said. "But you know how convincing my father can be. He told Mr. Daviet that he wouldn't have time to go again for another couple of weeks if they couldn't go today. And guess what? Mr. Daviet said he'd take them on a trail that's been closed because of the snow this winter. He wants to see if it's ready to be opened to other riders soon."

Stevie got a bad feeling in her stomach. Dinah, standing next to her and holding the reins, stiffened.

"What trail?" the two of them asked in a single voice.

"Rocky Road. Isn't that neat? I'm sure they're going to love it. It's such an exciting trail ride—or so I've heard."

Exciting. Yes, it was that, Stevie thought, depending on how one felt about tumbling rocks, landslides, and avalanches. That trail wasn't safe for an expert like Mr. Daviet, and it especially wasn't safe for novice riders like the Hales. Her mind suddenly filled with images of falling rocks, terrified horses, and wounded riders. The same thoughts had occurred to Dinah.

"They can't go!" Dinah said.

"Don't be silly. Of course they can," Betsy said. "Like I said, Dad told Mr. Daviet . . ."

"I don't mean they can't go riding; they can't go on Rocky Road."

"Why not?"

"It isn't safe!" Dinah said urgently.

Betsy seemed annoyed by Dinah's reaction. "I think Mr. Daviet's a better judge of that than you are," she snapped. "After all, if *he* thinks my parents—"

"That's not what I mean," Dinah said. Then she began talking quickly. "The trail isn't safe. I mean, it can't be safe at this time of year. All that snow melting is probably dislodging some of the boulders and rocks, and it could—" Dinah stopped talking because Betsy was staring at her.

"You were on it," Betsy said. "That's how you know."

Dinah stopped talking. She merely nodded.

"That's what happened, and you're hurt, aren't you?" Betsy asked.

"It was a big boulder," Dinah said finally. "It missed me by inches. Stevie saved me. The same thing could happen to your parents—only Stevie won't be there to save them. We can't let them go on the trail."

Betsy paled. "We've got to get back and warn them," she said, taking the reins from Dinah. "Hold on tight, or we won't get there in time! They're going out at eleven!"

Stevie looked at her watch. It was ten minutes to eleven. That didn't leave them much time at all. They were going to have to race.

Betsy slapped the horse's rump vigorously with the reins, and the lumbering old workhorse sparked to life.

"Hyaaa!" Betsy cried, turning him around as sharply as she dared. He responded.

"This isn't a sleek and speedy sleigh," Stevie said somewhat nervously.

Stevie gripped her seat.

Their trip into the forest had been at about two miles an hour. Their trip back to the Sugar Hut was much faster. The old horse finally got into a trot at Betsy's urging, and Stevie was surprised to see that he seemed to like it. He shook his head, loosening his mane, and seemed pleased to breath in some of the cool air. He snorted it out smartly.

Betsy didn't say anything for the whole trip. Stevie was sure her mind was brimming with questions, but every ounce of her concentration was focused on the horse, the sleigh, and the trail.

At the faster speed the trail seemed much more curvy and hilly than it had when they were going slowly. It swerved to the right and then turned sharply to the left.

"Hold on!" Dinah said.

"I *am* holding on!" Stevie replied.

"Not tight enough for this next curve!" she warned.

Betsy looked forward with grim determination on her face. Instead of slowing for the curve, she flicked the reins again. The horse's stride lengthened. They moved faster still. Stevie could feel her own fear mounting as they entered the turn. The horse kept to the right, then obediently began the turn to the left at breakneck speed, dragging the lumbering sleigh with its three passengers behind him.

The wood strained. Stevie could see it pressing into the horse's flesh as he made the turn. The next thing she felt was all the weight on the sleigh shifting dangerously to the left. She and Dinah automatically leaned to the right. Stevie didn't want to look at the horse anymore. She looked down at the snow. Just as they came to the point of the turn, the right runner of the sleigh actually pulled up out of the snow.

Stevie gasped. She also leaned farther to the right. The horse completed the turn, the sleigh straightened out, and both runners once again ran smoothly in the snow.

"There it is!" Betsy declared, looking straight ahead. Stevie looked up. It was the Sugar Hut. She looked at her watch. It was five minutes past eleven. Were they too late?

11

"I FIGURED IT out," Carole told Lisa as they sat in Colonel
Hanson's car on their way to Phil's pony club meeting.

"Figured *what* out?" Lisa asked. It always irritated her a
little bit when one of her friends started a sentence in the
middle of a thought and didn't take the time to tell her
what had come before. Stevie did it more than Carole,
but Carole was certainly doing it now.

"Mrs. Reg's story," Carole said.

Lisa recalled the rather mystifying tale of how Mrs.
Reg had taken care of somebody else's horse and the
horse had gotten to like her a lot. She hadn't yet made
sense of it. She wondered what Carole had seen that she
hadn't.

"In the first place," Carole went on, "she had heard what we were talking about."

"I know that," Lisa said. "Mrs. Reg may spend most of her time in her office, but it seems that her ears are all over the stable! She always hears everything."

"One of these days we've got to use that to our advantage," Carole said. "But that's not what she was talking about. What she was saying was that Stevie was away and, as Stevie's best friends, it's up to us to take care of Phil. See, while the owner of the horse was away, Mrs. Reg made friends with the horse, just so she could take care of it. But when the owner came back, although the horse was now attached to Mrs. Reg and not to him, he knew the horse had gotten good care and eventually would become reattached to him. That's why he wasn't angry with her."

"Oh," Lisa said, thinking about what it all meant. "You mean we're supposed to groom Phil and muck out his stall while Stevie's away?"

"No, not at all," Carole said, giggling at the idea. "We're supposed to be there when he needs a friend, i.e., at his pony club meeting. I don't know what this meeting is all about, but if he wants us there, we should be there. Get my drift?"

"I think I've got it," Lisa said. "Basically, it's okay for us to go in Stevie's place because we're trustworthy and honorable and her best friends and wouldn't want to steal her boyfriend anyway."

Colonel Hanson cleared his throat. The girls looked at him. "What do you think, Dad?" Carole asked.

"I think that if you tried to steal Stevie's boyfriend, she'd scratch your eyes out, so I'm sure it's the farthest thing from your minds."

"Definitely," Lisa confirmed.

"Just what I was thinking," Carole agreed.

Colonel Hanson drew the car to a stop and let the girls out at the stable where Phil's pony club, Cross County, had its meeting.

"Pick you up at one," he said.

"I NEED TO use the intercom," Betsy said breathlessly to an astonished Mrs. Daviet, dashing into the Sugar Hut. There was an intercom telephone in the Hut that connected with Sugarbush. Maybe it wasn't too late.

"That's only for my husband to use—"

Betsy didn't stop to argue. She grabbed the phone and pushed the code. Then she waited.

Stevie waited, too. She found herself flooded with emotions, including both fear and relief. She was afraid for the Hales and Mr. Daviet, but she was oddly relieved now that the secret she and Dinah had been keeping had come out. Usually Stevie loved secrets. This one, however, had been weighty and difficult. There would be consequences, of course, but they wouldn't be as bad as the consequences of not reaching Mr. Daviet in time.

"Mr. Daviet? You're still there?" Betsy said, relief flooding her voice.

Stevie let out her breath, unaware that she'd even been holding it.

"I'll tell him," Dinah said, reaching for the phone. Betsy handed it to her and stepped back, waiting.

"We shouldn't have done it, Mr. Daviet," she began. "I don't want to get anybody in trouble. It was all my fault—"

There was a brief silence. Dinah's face reddened. But then she took a deep breath and began at the beginning.

With each word Stevie could feel a weight lifting from her. It was the last thing she would have expected to feel when a secret came out, but she definitely felt better listening to Dinah tell everything they had done.

Finally Dinah hung up the phone. She sat down on a wooden bench, leaned back against the rough-hewn wall, and began crying uncontrollably. She was still crying when her parents, summoned by Mr. Daviet, arrived to take her to the doctor.

"MRS. REG! MRS. REG!" Lisa called out eagerly when she and Carole returned to Pine Hollow after Phil's pony club meeting.

"What is it, child?" Mrs. Reg asked, emerging from

the feed room where she had been overseeing the blending of grains.

"Thank you!" Lisa gave the woman a hug. Mrs. Reg was more than a little bit astonished by the thanks, but she hugged back nevertheless.

"Whatever for?" she asked, finally.

"For telling Carole and me that we should go to Phil's pony club meeting. It was wonderful. You won't believe it! Stevie would have killed us if we hadn't been there. You were exactly right!"

"Me? What are you talking about? I don't know anything about Phil's pony club, and just who is Phil?"

"Phil Marston, you know, Stevie's boyfriend?"

"Stevie has a boyfriend?" Mrs. Reg asked. She seemed genuinely surprised. When Lisa paused to think about it, however, she knew that Mrs. Reg knew perfectly well who Phil was. He'd ridden at Pine Hollow several times. Although Mrs. Reg might, occasionally, forget a boyfriend, she'd never forget a rider.

"You didn't exactly tell us right out," Carole said, coming up behind Lisa to give her support. "You just told us that story about the man whose mare you took care of. Remember, the horse who got so attached to you?"

"Hmmm," Mrs. Reg said. Obviously she wasn't going to admit that there was any connection. That was just like her. "I never forget a horse," she said. "That one was one of my favorites."

"Hmmmm," Carole said, echoing Mrs. Reg. "I'm beginning to think that mare was one of mine, too. So anyway, thanks, Mrs. Reg."

"I'm glad you had such fun," Mrs. Reg said. "Now it seems to me that there are a couple of stalls to muck out before class begins. . . ."

"Tallyho!" Carole responded eagerly, picking up a pitchfork.

"Yoicks!" Lisa agreed.

12

"STEVIE, WE'LL SEE you later," Mrs. Slattery said, dimissing her. Stevie opened the car door and went into the Slatterys' house. Mr. Slattery drove off, taking Dinah to her doctor's appointment.

Stevie definitely felt relieved that the secret was out, especially since it meant Dinah would finally see a doctor. Still she felt an uncomfortable foreboding. There were good reasons why they'd originally kept the secret. For one thing, Jodi was in trouble. Today was her day off at Sugarbush, but Mr. Daviet had grumbled that he was going to call her at home. Stevie and Dinah had both insisted that Jodi was not to blame, but that didn't seem to mean much to him. He'd kept on grumbling. He'd also scowled at Dinah. If there was one thing Mr. Daviet and Max had in common, it was their feelings about the rules of safety in riding. Going on the Rocky Road Trail had definitely violated those rules. It had endangered his riders and his horses. He wasn't going to forget that.

Another important reason they'd kept the secret was Dinah's conviction that her parents would tell her she couldn't ride anymore. This was about the worst thing Stevie could imagine. Why couldn't the Slatterys be more like the Hales, joining in on their daughters' activities, Stevie wondered, or like her own parents, more or less ignoring the activities unless they interfered with schoolwork?

Stevie went up to Dinah's room and changed her clothes, slipping into some clean dry jeans, a turtleneck, and a sweatshirt. All the while she was thinking about Dinah's dilemma. What she realized, the more she thought about it, was that if she hadn't been there, it never would have happened. Dinah wouldn't have been able to go out on any trail ride at all, much less the Rocky Road. So if she'd been the one to get Dinah into all this trouble, she'd have to be the one to get her out of it.

Stevie looked at herself squarely in the mirror. She arranged her face so it looked serious, sincere. It didn't look a lot like Stevie, but it looked *earnest*.

"Mrs. Slattery," she began. "It wasn't Dinah's fault. You shouldn't punish her. You know my reputation as a troublemaker, and it's all true. Dinah didn't want to go on the trail. I was the one . . ."

No, that wouldn't do at all. Stevie certainly did have a reputation as a troublemaker, but she had no reputation at all as a martyr. The Slatterys would never believe it.

"Horseback riding isn't just a sport, or just a lot of fun," she began, trying another tack. "Although it is those things, it's an activity that builds character and develops responsibility. . . ."

Except in Stevie and Dinah, it seemed. She decided that wouldn't do, either.

"We knew we weren't supposed to do it," Stevie said, beginning over. "We just didn't consider the consequences." That, at least, had the advantage of being true. "We thought the trail was closed because of the sugaring off. We didn't consider the fact that it was closed because it was dangerous." That, too, was true. However, it left unanswered the question of how it was that they'd been allowed to go on a trail ride by themselves in the first place. That led Stevie to think about Jodi. She didn't like the thoughts she had about Jodi, and she was beginning to realize that she didn't like Jodi.

She'd dismissed Betsy's complaints about her sister as complaints about a big sister, but in this case Stevie was getting the idea that maybe Betsy knew more about Jodi than either she or Dinah did. Dinah adored Jodi, but why?

Stevie had a feeling that she knew the answer. Dinah

adored Jodi because Jodi was everything Dinah wasn't. Jodi was older. She had a lot of horseback riding experience. She could spend just about all day every day at Sugarbush Stables because she worked there. She also was somebody who didn't think much of rules. She broke them a lot. She didn't see anything wrong with offering a "lesson" to a boy when she didn't intend to teach him anything—at least she didn't intend to teach him anything about tack!

Dinah wasn't like that. She liked to have fun, but she wasn't a rule breaker, not even as much as Stevie was. Stevie liked her because they always had good times together, not because Dinah was any goody-two-shoes. Stevie knew Dinah had missed her when she moved to Vermont. Maybe Dinah had thought that Stevie and Jodi were alike and she'd admired Jodi for that reason.

But we're not alike, Stevie told herself. I'm not afraid of getting into a little bit of trouble, but I'd never do anything unsafe—unless I had to. Well, she relented, not anything *really* unsafe. Besides, although Stevie occasionally took risks she didn't have to, she'd never tell anybody else to do something that was unsafe.

That was the problem. If Jodi had gone out on the trail by herself or with them, that would have been one thing. The fact was that Jodi had let them go out by themselves, knowing that the trail had been closed because it was always unsafe in the winter.

That wasn't just dangerous, that was reckless. And they'd been covering for her.

Stevie looked back up at the mirror. "Mrs. Slattery," she began, "we should have known better. It was a really stupid thing to do. Just because somebody else says something is all right doesn't mean that we should go along with them. I'm sorry. I'm truly sorry."

That was the truth. It was that simple.

The Slatterys' car pulled into the driveway. Dinah climbed carefully out of the backseat. Stevie descended the stairs quickly. She wanted to talk to the Slatterys before they lowered the boom on Dinah.

"Are you okay?" she asked Dinah.

"Yes, I'm fine," her friend replied. "In fact, the doctor admired the leg wrap. I thought you'd want to kow that." She smiled. Stevie felt terribly relieved. She turned to Dinah's parents.

"Mr. and Mrs. Slattery, there's something I need to say," she began. "This wasn't Dinah's fault, really. It was mostly mine. It wouldn't have happened if I hadn't been here."

"Thanks, Stevie," Mr. Slattery said. "Dinah told us everything. We have an idea where the fault lies. We understand what the two of you were doing and why you were doing it.

"We even appreciate the fact that it must have been hard to come clean this morning when you learned what was at stake. We wish both of you had known you could trust us and had told us right away. Most of all, though, we're relieved to know no serious damage was done. We're also pretty sure nothing like this will ever happen again."

"You mean you're not going to punish Dinah?" Stevie asked.

"No, we don't mean that," Mr. Slattery said.

Stevie's heart sank.

"Dinah won't be allowed to ride for a month," he told Stevie. "I mean a month *after* all her cuts and bruises heal."

A *month?* It seemed like a lifetime, but it wasn't; it was just a month. Dinah would be riding again before summer!

Stevie tried not to look too happy. After all, she didn't want the Slatterys to get the idea that she didn't think that was a harsh punishment.

"I want to change my clothes now," Dinah said. "Help me upstairs, will you?" she asked Stevie. Stevie was only too happy to do so. She had to get out of there before she grinned!

"Isn't it great?" Dinah asked as soon as the door to her room was closed. "It was all I could do to keep from cheering. I was just sure they'd tell me I couldn't ride at all. My parents are really okay."

"It's almost too bad you didn't get a chance to hear the speech I've been working on since I got home. It's a convincing one, but it centers a lot on the idea that banning you from horseback riding for the rest of your life is too cruel. There's even a point in it where I suggest that a year would be sufficient!"

"Keep it to yourself!" Dinah said. She put on some clean clothes and then the two girls collapsed on the twin beds in the room in total relief.

"I've been thinking about Jodi," Stevie began hesitantly.

"Me, too," Dinah said.

"I've been thinking that she was wrong, too."

"You bet she was," Dinah said, anger rising in her voice. It surprised Stevie, who had expected that Dinah would defend Jodi.

"She shouldn't have let us go out on the trail, and she shouldn't have asked us to keep the secret."

"That, too," Dinah said.

"What else?" Stevie asked.

"What she said to me that night . . . ," Dinah began. Stevie thought back to the cool night outside the Sugar Hut when the clearing was filled with all the kids playing Frisbee by moonlight. Everybody there was laughing and having fun—everybody except Dinah.

"Is that what made you cry?" Stevie asked.

Dinah nodded. Stevie could tell from the way she was talking that even now the memory was painful. She didn't cry, however. She just talked.

"Jodi found me outside, behind that tree. She'd figured the reason we'd gone outside was because I didn't want to take off any overclothes and show my cuts. I guess she was afraid I'd change my mind, so she came over to convince me it wouldn't be a good idea to change my mind."

"What did she say that upset you so much?" Stevie asked.

"She told me that if I told anybody, she'd see to it that I'd never ride Goldie again. She also said that I probably didn't deserve to ride Goldie anyway because if I couldn't stay on a horse like Goldie, I was never going to be a good rider. I had this awful picture of spending the rest of my life riding in circles in a little ring. I'm on a pony and Jodi Hale has the lead rope. It was just awful! She swore it was going to happen, too!"

"That's so mean!" Stevie said. "No wonder you were crying. And no wonder you didn't want to tell me. Well, let me tell you something: I may not be the best rider in the world, but I'm pretty good, and I've had a lot of experience. Just about nobody could have stayed on Goldie at that moment. If a horse is totally determined to lose his rider, he's going to lose his rider, and I never saw a horse more determined than Goldie was right then. I couldn't have stayed on him. Even Carole Hanson would have gone flying. The miracle was that you stayed on through that trememdous rear. You were fabulous!"

"I was?" Dinah looked astonished.

"You were. And you are." Stevie gave her a very careful hug. "You'll be riding again soon, and you'll be better than ever. And if I'm any judge of sap, you may even be riding Goldie."

"You think so?"

Stevie nodded. Then she shrugged. "Let's put it this way: I *hope* so."

"You know what the best news is about today's whole mess?" Dinah asked.

"You'll be riding before summer," Stevie said.

"Maybe, but even before that, the best news is that I won't have to wear my hair over half my face anymore!"

"You don't like the latest hairstyle à la Mademoiselle Stevie?" Stevie asked, pretending to be hurt. Then she shifted into the character of Mademoiselle Stevie. "Wees zees air-style, Mademoiselle Dinah could be zee belle of zee balle, eef only zare were a balle to be a belle of!"

"Oh, but there is!" Dinah declared, her eyes suddenly lighting up in realization.

"A ball?" Stevie asked, reverting to her usual self.

"Yes, tonight is the annual Sugaring Off Square Dance!"

They had both completely forgotten all about it. Now they had only a few hours to get ready. Dinah headed for her closet; Stevie made a beeline for the curling iron.

Sugarbush Stables seemed to have been completely transformed. Stevie almost didn't recognize it when she got there that night with Dinah and her family for the Sugaring Off Square Dance. For one thing, the outside of the stable was festooned with hanging lanterns. It looked downright summery—except for all the snow on the ground. The lamps swayed in the gentle breeze, and the light danced invitingly on the snow.

The girls had spent the afternoon and early evening putting together their outfits for the night, when they weren't on the phone with Betsy, explaining everything. As the whole story unraveled, Stevie and Dinah felt awful about a lot of things, but the worst part was having lied to a friend.

"I was worried," Betsy said. "I knew something was wrong, but I didn't know what." She told them she'd also suspected Jodi was part of it. "That made it even worse because anything to do with Jodi that's a secret has got to be bad news. I'm just glad it came out all right."

"You're not angry with me?" Dinah asked.

"No," Betsy assured her. "How could I be? In spite of everything, with Stevie on our team, I think we've got a chance to win. Who needs you?" she teased. "Anyway, I know that what you did wasn't easy. Keeping a secret is tough, but it's not as tough as letting it out. You might have just saved my parents, and Mr. Daviet. I ought to be thanking you."

"You're welcome, but I promise we'll never do it again."

"Deal," Betsy said. "See you tonight!"

Stevie and Dinah then turned their attention to their makeovers, or in Dinah's case, her *un*makeover. Although Stevie was most comfortable in jeans, and felt that they were appropriate for a square dance, Dinah had convinced her that it would be more fun to have a skirt that could swing to the music while she sashayed across the dance floor. Dinah herself wore jeans. She could go to the dance and have fun, but she was still much too sore to swing with a partner.

Although Stevie had wanted to try some new hairdos for both of them—she was inclined toward long bouncing sausage curls because it seemed sort of Early American—Dinah had talked her out of it. Both of them ended up looking remarkably normal, not counting the fact that a skirt wasn't "normal" for Stevie.

As soon as they got out of the car, they hurried into the barn, normally a storage area for the stables. Tonight the entire floor had been cleared of tractors, wagons, and sleighs. In their place were more than a hundred people, a great big long table full of refreshments, and a real country square-dance band.

"Now, everybody grab a partner," the caller insisted. Before Stevie even had a chance to wonder whom she might dance with, one of the boys who'd been in on her Frisbee game came up and took her hand.

"If you can dance as well as you catch a pie plate, we're going to have fun," he said, introducing himself as Michael.

"We'll just see," Stevie said, following him to join three other couples on the dance floor to make a square.

Stevie had been at square dances, but never when it felt as authentic as this one did. For instance, she'd never been at a square dance on a winter night in a barn. It should have been cold, but the place was warmed by the presence of all the people and the animals who lived below. The smell of sweet hay permeated the place. There was also the pleasant smell of the regular tenants. As far as Stevie was concerned, the two best smells in the world were horses and hay. She was quite content. Of course, it might have been more perfect if she had Phil there. . . .

The caller explained the dance they were about to do and had one of the squares demonstrate.

"Ready?" he asked.

Michael winked at Stevie. She winked back. The dance began. At first the caller went through the dance slowly, letting the dancers get the idea of what they were doing. The second time through it was a little faster, and the third time through they were flying! When it was over, Michael suggested they get something to drink, and Stevie was very happy to see that the refreshment table had an ample supply of cider.

The problem was that Stevie barely had a chance to take a sip before another one of her Frisbee mates came and asked her to dance. How could she say no? She guzzled down the rest of the cider and returned to the dance floor for the next set.

Dinah found a soft seat and moved it behind the refreshment table. Even though she couldn't dance, she could help the dancers by keeping the cider cups filled.

It seemed that everybody in town was at the dance, and, Stevie thought, everybody wanted to dance with her. It wasn't exactly true. The fact was that there were more men there than women, so just about all the women danced every dance. That was fine with Stevie. She was having a wonderful time.

"May I have this dance?" a man behind her asked. Stevie turned and was surprised to see that it was Mr. Daviet. She could feel herself blushing. Mr. Daviet was one of the people who had been hurt by their secret. He was a nice man. It hadn't been fair to him.

"You really want to dance with me?" she said.

"Certainly, I do. I want to ask you about the miracle cure you got for your recovery from surgery."

"Surgery?"

"Your leg," he said. "If I recall correctly, you had surgery on a leg recently. Betsy told me all about it when she asked if you three could take the sleigh to put out your buckets."

It all came back to Stevie. So much had happened since that first day that she had completely forgotten about the little fib her friends had told.

"Fresh air," she replied quickly. "Like I told you, it's the best medicine there is. Plus exercise. Shall we dance?"

He smiled at her and nodded. "I suspected a miracle cure in the offing when the girls described the surgery to me. I was going to offer you the sled anyway. Since you've never been on snowshoes before, you would have been at a terrible disadvantage. Now, let's go," he said, offering Stevie his arm. They went off to do-si-do in style.

Finally the band took a little break, and Stevie wasn't

sorry for a chance to sit down and chat with Dinah. "This is just wonderful," she said.

"Ah, and the best part is yet to come," Dinah said rather mysteriously. Stevie liked the sound of it. She was about to ask Dinah what she meant when she heard Dinah's name being spoken harshly.

Stevie turned. There was Jodi Hale. She was at the dance, but she wasn't dressed up for it. She stood in front of Dinah defiantly. A young man, Stevie thought she recognized him as Mark, Jodi's "student," was with her.

"Proud of yourself?" Jodi demanded.

"It was to help your parents," Dinah said. She was clearly uncomfortable with a confrontation. Up until a few hours earlier, Jodi had been somebody she'd admired enough to get into real trouble for. "Your parents could have gotten badly hurt—just like I was."

"They are better riders than you are, or than you'll ever be. They could have been just fine," Jodi told her. "The rocks fall on that trail sometimes, but not all the time. What was the big deal?"

The big deal? Stevie could hardly believe her ears. She kept quiet, though. This was between Dinah and Jodi.

Dinah stood up from her stool without showing the pain she felt throughout her body. "Jodi, I used to think that all I wanted in the world was to be just like you," she began. "I admired you more than anybody else I knew. I tried to be like you, but I have found in the last few days that I just can't do it. I also don't *want* to do it. There are differences between us. For one thing, I know the difference between right and wrong. I also know the difference between safe and sorry. For a while I forgot those things, but now I remember, and I'm not going to forget them again."

Jodi put her hands on her hips defiantly. "There are other differences between us," she said. "The biggest one is that you'll never be a good rider if you can't stay on a skittish horse. I'll always be better than you are." She spun on her heel, then looked back at her boyfriend. "Come on, Mark, let's get out of here." They left without saying another word.

Dinah's face reddened in anger and resentment. Stevie wanted to reach out and comfort her. She was very proud of her friend and what she'd said to Jodi. She also knew that, in spite of her assurances earlier, Jodi's words stung.

It was Mr. Daviet who came to Dinah's rescue then. Stevie and Dinah hadn't realized that he'd seen the confrontation. He hadn't missed a word. "If it's any comfort to you, Dinah, you should know that Jodi's future riding will not take place at Sugarbush. You did something you shouldn't have done, but Jodi did something inexcusable, and that was to put some of my riders at risk. Even worse, she asked you to cover up for her. She won't be on any of my horses again. Ever. You, however, will have many opportunities to continue riding there. I'm glad of it. You're a good student. I wish I had more like you. For one thing, you keep your head in an emergency. Now, the trick is to avoid emergencies in the future!"

Dinah stammered. She didn't know what to say. She was spared having to say anything by the return of the band. The moment the music started, Mr. Slattery asked Stevie to dance. She was pleased to accept.

The dancing continued nonstop for another half hour, and then Mr. Daviet stood up on the bandstand.

"Your attention, please," he said. "We have a few little ceremonial items to go through, and then we can return to dancing. First of all, as many of you know, Mrs. Daviet has been over at the Sugar Hut finishing the evaporation process on the final batch of sap. She's also been cooking down some of the first batch of sap to make our first batch of sugar. It's our tradition here to have our first sugar sampled by our newest worker. I have the sugar here, so will our newest worker come to the bandstand?"

Stevie looked around the room. What she saw was that everybody was looking at her.

"Me?" she said, looking quizzically at Mr. Daviet.

"Of course," he said. "Besides, you've got to have something sweet to replenish all the energy you used so you can go on dancing for the rest of the night. Come on up here!"

Stevie walked slowly through the crowd, receiving

good wishes and pats on the back as she went. She hadn't expected this, and she wished Dinah had warned her.

Soon she was standing next to Mr. Daviet. Mrs. Daviet arrived with a platter filled with little chunks of maple sugar, sweet smelling and hot.

"Be our guest," he said.

Stevie took a piece. It was hot, piping hot.

"Ouch!" she said.

There was laughter. "You thought this was an honor," Mr. Daviet teased. "The truth is, we just want to let a stranger burn her fingers. We're too smart for that!"

Stevie held the morsel on the palm of her hand and blew on it. There was silence in the barn. She held the morsel out to the crowd. "Blow," she instructed. They did.

When she judged that it just might be cool enough, she tested it with the tip of her tongue. It wasn't quite cool enough, but it was so sweet and inviting, she couldn't resist. She took a nibble. It did burn her tongue, but she didn't care. It was the sweetest, most wonderful thing she'd ever tasted. She'd had maple sugar before, but she'd never had it piping hot and fresh. It was wonderful, and she told everybody so.

The crowd applauded, and then Mrs. Daviet and her assistants began walking through the crowd, passing out morsels to everybody who wanted it—and that was everybody there.

Then, while the guests were still testing the sugar, Mr. Daviet pulled a piece of paper out of his pocket.

"Oh, there's one more thing here," he said. "All of the sap was gathered by my junior riders, and in order to get them to do a lot of work for free, I make it a sort of contest."

The adults laughed. So did the kids.

"Anyway, Mrs. Daviet has finished tallying up the amount of sap that was brought in by each of the teams of three students, and the team that brought in the most sap is guaranteed to have first pick of horses for classes all summer."

He glanced at the piece of paper and then put it back into his pocket.

"All my horses are great animals," he said. "And they're all different. Some are fast, some have good canters, some have smooth trots, and some are pretty. Some are even gentle."

There was laughter. He looked at the paper again and then tucked it back into his pocket.

"The kids gathered a lot of sap this year, and as you can tell from tonight's sampling, it's making high-quality maple products. We couldn't do it without the help of our young riders. . . ."

Stevie thought this talk would never end. Mr. Daviet went on for what seemed like hours, but was really probably just a few minutes. The suspense was just about unbearable.

". . . and so it's always hard to recognize just *one* team when all of them work so hard . . ."

He went on to describe exactly what the teams did. He checked the paper again. Then he put it into his pocket again. Stevie thought it was getting frayed.

". . . but the fact is, one team did do better than the others . . ."

This led to a discussion of the benefits of having a contest. It did not lead directly to the announcement of the winner.

". . . and the winner is . . . a team who worked hard, in spite of difficulties . . ."

Just when Stevie thought she couldn't stand the tension and the buildup for one more second, Mr. Daviet did it.

". . . the winning team is Dinah Slattery, Betsy Hale, and our newcomer Stevie Lake!"

They'd done it! They'd won! Stevie felt her self bursting with a feeling of total joy.

Nearby Betsy was jumping up and down excitedly. Behind the refreshment table, Dinah was stunned. Soundlessly she said the one thing that was on her mind. Stevie couldn't hear it, but she saw the word forming on her friend's lips.

"Goldie!"

14

STEVIE HAD LOVED almost every minute of her trip to Vermont. The one thing that had been missing—two things, actually—were Carole and Lisa. She got home too late Sunday night to call, and she couldn't see them all day Monday because she was at school. When the final bell sounded, she couldn't get to Pine Hollow fast enough. She knew she'd find them there. They were in the paddock, where Carole was working Starlight on a lunge line. The minute they saw Stevie, Carole secured Starlight, and the three of them had an impromptu Saddle Club meeting—their first in over a week.

"Oh, Stevie! We're so glad you're back! We have the most wonderful news!" Lisa greeted her.

Carole gave her a hug. "It's a big secret, see, but you're going to love it!" she said.

Stevie groaned. "I don't want to hear about secrets. They can get you into real trouble, so whatever it is, you're just better off telling other people and letting them help. You just never know about secrets. They're no good and that's that."

Carole and Lisa exchanged glances. "Is this Stevie Lake in front of us, or was there some kind of extraterrestrial bodily exchange while she was in Vermont?" Lisa asked.

"Maybe just a Vulcan mind-swap," Carole said. "After all, the Stevie we know loves secrets more than anything in the world—especially when she can tell them!"

"And we can tell this one," Lisa said.

"You can?" Stevie was very wary of secrets, but if something could be told, then it wouldn't be a secret anymore, and that would be okay.

"Sure."

"Then tell," she said.

"When we called Phil and told him you couldn't come to the pony club meeting, like you asked us to, he told us *we* should come instead," Carole said.

"We weren't sure whether you would think it was okay," Lisa said uncertainly. "But Mrs. Reg told us this story—"

"Oh, come on, Lisa," Carole said. "Stevie doesn't care about that old mare. She's going to be much more interested in the meeting."

"If you'll ever tell me what it was about," Stevie said pointedly. In her opinion, when it was time to share secrets, they should be shared, not just hinted at.

"Oh, right," Lisa said. "Well, it turns out that Phil was really glad we called because it was sort of an organizational meeting . . . and only people who were there, or represented there, can be involved. . . ."

"In what?" Stevie shrieked. "Tell me!"

"Does the word 'tallyho' mean anything to you?" Carole asked.

Stevie could hardly believe it. "A hunt?" she asked. "There's going to be a fox hunt?"

"And we can be there!" Lisa said.

"It's going to be at Cross County. I guess it's an annual hunt for all the young riders and this time they can invite friends, too!" Carole said.

"And that means us?" Stevie asked.

Her friends nodded.

"Now I understand why Phil was so insistent that I be at the meeting. Boy, am I glad you guys called him and went. Wouldn't it have been *awful* if we couldn't have gone just because I was away? Oh, fabulous!"

Lisa and Carole filled her in on some of the specifics and told her there would be another organizational meeting the following week. They all agreed they would be there—with bells on.

"No, in pink jackets," Stevie said excitedly, recalling pictures of hunters wearing red jackets that were somehow called pink.

"Did you know that's not actually pink?" Carole asked.

"Sure, they're red," Stevie said. "I still don't know why they're called pink, though."

"It's P-i-n-q-u-e," Carole said, spelling it out. "It doesn't have anything to do with the color. Pinque was the tailor who designed it."

"There's so much to learn!" Lisa said.

"And we're going to have so much fun learning it," Stevie said.

"Speaking of learning new things," Lisa said. "Tell us all about making maple syrup."

Stevie grinned. "I thought you'd *never* ask," she said. "Now I'll begin at the beginning. . . ."

And she did.

ABOUT THE AUTHOR

BONNIE BRYANT is the author of more than fifty books for young readers, including novelizations of movie hits such as *Teenage Mutant Ninja Turtles* and *Honey, I Shrunk the Kids*, written under her married name, B. B. Hiller.

Ms. Bryant began writing The Saddle Club in 1986. Although she had done some riding before that, she intensified her studies then and found herself learning right along with her characters Stevie, Carole, and Lisa. She claims that they are all much better riders than she is.

Ms. Bryant was born and raised in New York City. She lives in Greenwich Village with her two sons.

T·H·E
SADDLE CLUB

A blue-ribbon series by Bonnie Bryant

Stevie, Carole and Lisa are all very different, but they *love* horses! The three girls are best friends at Pine Hollow Stables, where they ride and care for all kinds of horses. Come to Pine Hollow and get ready for all the fun and adventure that comes with being 13!

Watch for other SADDLE CLUB books all year. More great reading—and riding to come!